PARK'S QUEST

Park wanted to know how and why his father died—even when. Deceased: January 22, 1973. It seemed plain enough until you begin to think about time zones. That would have been a different day in America, or had they figured it in when they set the date? He needed to know stupid little things like that.

Not to mention bigger things. For instance, if he, Park, was Parkington Waddell Broughton the Fifth, then there had been not only a fourth, but a third, a second, a first. . . . Maybe his father might still be alive. Park shivered at the thought.

KATHERINE PATERSON

PARK'S QUEST

PUFFIN BOOKS

PUFFIN BOOKS
A Division of Penguin Books USA Inc.

375 Hudson Street, New York, New York 10014
Penguin Books Ltd, 27 Wrights Lane, London W8 5TZ, England
Penguin Books Australia Ltd, Ringwood, Victoria, Australia
Penguin Books Canada Ltd, 10 Alcorn Avenue, Toronto, Ontario, Canada M4V 3B2
Penguin Books (N.Z.) Ltd, 182–190 Wairau Road, Auckland 10, New Zealand

Penguin Books Ltd, Registered Offices: Harmondsworth, Middlesex, England

First published in the United States of America by E.P. Dutton,
a division of Penguin Books USA Inc., 1988
Published in Puffin Books, 1989
     14   16   18   20   19   17   15
Copyright © Katherine Paterson, 1988
The author and publisher gratefully acknowledge permission to reprint:
the epigraphs on page 3
From *The Sword and the Circle* by Rosemary Sutcliff.
Copyright © 1981 by Rosemary Sutcliff. Reprinted by permission of the
publisher, E. P. Dutton, a division of Penguin Books USA Inc.
From "To Heal a Nation" by Joel L. Swerdlow. *National Geographic*, May 1985,
Vol. 167, No. 5. Reprinted with the permission of *National Geographic*.
And from *To Heal a Nation* by Joel L. Swerdlow. Copyright © 1985,
Joel L. Swerdlow. Reprinted with the permission of
the William Morris Agency, Inc. On behalf of the author.
the poem on page 19 and page 20, top
Reprinted by permission of the publishers and Trustees of Amherst College
from *The Poems of Emily Dickinson*, edited by Thomas H. Johnson,
Cambridge, Mass.: The Belknap Press of Harvard University Press,
Copyright © 1951, 1955, 1979, 1983 by The President and Fellows of Harvard College.

No character in this book is intended to represent any actual
person; all the incidents of the story are entirely fictional in nature.

LIBRARY OF CONGRESS CATALOGING-IN-PUBLICATION DATA
Paterson, Katherine.   Park's quest / Katherine Paterson.   p.   cm.
    "First published in the United States of America by E.P. Dutton, a
division of Penguin Books USA Inc., 1988"—verso t.p.
    Summary: Eleven-year-old Park makes some startling discoveries
when he travels to his grandfather's farm in Virginia to learn about
his father who died in the Vietnam War.
    ISBN 0-14-034262-1
    [1. Farm life—Fiction.   2. Vietnamese Americans—Fiction.]   I. Title.
[PZ7.P273Par   1989]   [Fic]—dc20   89-33407

Printed in the United States of America   Set in Garamond #3

for
Kathryn Harris Morton
and those round her table
Tim, Eleanor, Hank, Anne, Irene
and
the two Kenneths
whose name was written on
the Siege Perilous

CONTENTS

PARK'S
QUEST

"We shall come together again," said Lancelot, trying to console him.

"Some of us," said the King. "But it will not be the same; never the same again. . . . We shall have served our purpose; made a shining time between the Dark and the Dark. Merlin said that it would be as though all things drew on to the golden glory of the sunset. But then it will all be over."

Lancelot said, "We shall have made such a blaze, that men will remember us on the other side of the Dark."

Rosemary Sutcliff
The Sword and the Circle

The names have a power, a life, all their own. Even on the coldest days, sunlight makes them warm to the touch. Young men put into the earth, rising out of the earth. You can feel their blood flowing again.

Everyone, including those who knew no one who served in Vietnam, seems to touch the stone. Lips say a name over and over, and then stretch up to kiss it. Fingertips trace letters.

Perhaps by touching, people renew their faith in love and in life; or perhaps they better understand sacrifice and sorrow.

"We're with you," they say. "We will never forget."

Joel L. Swerdlow
"To Heal a Nation"

PARKINGTON WADDELL BROUGHTON THE FIFTH

·1·

Casually he draped the dish towel over his shoulder. Now the left hand gripped an invisible shield and, balancing the soup ladle in the right, the boy turned slowly and took dead aim at the heart of the refrigerator.

"Faugh! You are no knight!" the lady cried in disgust. "You are naught but a kitchen scullion, smelling of garlic and grease. How dare you presume to be my champion? Dismount, fool, and stand aside, lest the Black Knight skewer you on his spear and roast you in the everlasting flames!"

Bold Gareth heeded not the lady's jeers, but put his

spear at rest and rode full gallop at the Black Knight's shield. The very hooves of his war-horse seemed to fly above the earth as he charged like an avenging angel in full flight, shattering his opponent's spear. The Black Knight crashed heavily to the earth. Noble Gareth leapt from his horse and, raising his sword . . .

"Pork!"
All one hundred forty pounds of him had landed, and the dishes were still rattling in the drain.
"What on earth?"

He turned slowly to look at her, the arrogant lady. Had she not fallen on her knees and pled with the King to send a knight to kill this villain for her? And the noble Arthur had chosen him for the quest, ending his year of humble service in the kitchens of Camelot. Gareth turned from her sneering face and raised his sword above the fallen foe. "Cry for mercy, you perfidious creature!"

His mother sighed. "Just don't jump around in here, all right? That ladle"—she took it out of his hands—"is *not* a weapon."
He smiled at her indulgently. They were nearly the same height.
"Basketball moves, right?"

Basketball moves. Alas, that his true identity must remain concealed from the ungrateful wench. How she will reel in mortification when she learns that he whom she insults is in very truth the son of the King of Orkney and nephew to the mighty Arthur himself. "Forsooth, churl . . ."

"Yoo-hoo. Pork. This is your mother speaking. Finish drying the dishes and then get to your homework." Randy took the empty soup pot off the stove and attacked it with steel wool. "Yoo-hoo. Can you hear me?"

He turned and bowed slightly. "I am at your service," he murmured. "And at the King's."

Without another word, he removed the black armor from the fallen knight and clothed himself in it. Henceforward no one would mistake him for a kitchen drudge. He was ready now for whatever enchantments the wicked queen Morgana le Fay might devise in her evil imaginings. He mounted once more, calling to the dwarf to follow.

Park hung up the dish towel and, in one practiced movement, slid out of the tiny kitchen, flipped the television switch, and flopped onto the living room couch.

"Pork!" Maybe if he didn't answer, she'd stop calling him by his baby name.

She stuck her head into the room. "No TV until all the homework is done, my friend."

"Holiday," he muttered.

"What?"

He didn't answer. On the news they were showing the crowds gathering in the city. Washington was full and running over with veterans. Men in all kinds of uniforms in all stages of wear and tear. A peroxide blonde reporter was interviewing a man in tattered fatigues with a chest full of medals. The camera moved slightly to show that the man had his hair braided in a pigtail that went halfway down his back. Weird.

"Pork?" She had come out and was leaning against the

7

doorway, the pot and the steel wool still in her hands, her eyes on the TV.

"How about that, Mom? Millions of people. From all over everywhere."

"I see."

He cleared his throat and, without looking at her, said in a carefully casual tone, "Why don't we go down tomorrow? You and me?"

"No." She said the word sharply, adding more gently, "I have to work."

"On Veterans Day?"

She waved the steel wool at the crowds on the screen. "Thalhimers is hoping to relieve them of some of their money."

"Yeah, well, how about"—he still didn't meet her eyes— "how about if just I go?"

"No."

Now Park looked her in the face. Her eyes were jiggling. He could tell she was trying to make up a reason fast. "A crowd like that? You could see everything much better on TV." She was warming to her excuse. "Remember when we tried to go to the inauguration? We said 'never again.' Remember?"

"This is different. It wasn't my dad being inaugurated." There, he'd said it. Right out in the open. Let her deal with that.

She went over and snapped off the set. "It's not safe. I'd worry all day." She turned back toward the kitchen, not looking him in the eye.

"Homework." She gave his knee a light slap as she passed.

"It's a holiday, Mom. I told you."

She was in the kitchen. Park could hear her emptying the dishwater and imagine her scrubbing the sink and the

8

counter, her knuckles white with the effort. It never really looked clean, no matter how hard she tried.

"Mom?" he called over his shoulder toward her. "When did he ever actually see me?"

"Who?"

"My dad. Did he ever see me?"

"Well, of course he saw you." She sounded impatient. "You were three, four months old when he came back. How many times do I have to tell you?"

"And?"

"What do you mean 'and'?"

"What did he think?"

"I've *told* you that. He thought you looked exactly like Porky Pig."

It didn't seem fair that practically the only gift his father had given him was a nickname he despised. "I wish you wouldn't keep calling me Pork."

There was a hesitation. "You don't seriously want me to go around calling you Parkington Waddell Broughton the Fifth, do you?"

"Why don't you just call me Park like everybody else?"

Another pause. "That was *his* name."

Park got up and went to the kitchen door. He was eleven now. She couldn't keep on putting off his questions, telling him he was too young to understand. She had her head in the refrigerator, so he found himself talking mostly to her rear end. Well, he couldn't let that stop him. "How come," he asked, "I mean, if my dad was in 'Nam when I was born and he saw me after I was born—how come he was back there again when he got killed? I don't get it." He waited a minute, but the back did not answer. "I mean people just went to 'Nam for one year. That's a known fact. How come my dad—?"

She straightened abruptly. "*Why?* I just want to know *why* you insist on putting empty milk cartons into the fridge. I always think we have milk, and then—" She turned on him accusingly, shaking the half-gallon carton in his face. "There's no milk for breakfast. How old are you? I would think—" Boy, she was good at changing the subject.

He took the carton from her and pitched it toward the trash basket. It missed. Some basketball player. In one step he took the entire width of the floor and scooped the carton into the trash. "I'll go get some," he said.

She got her purse and gave him a dollar. She was smiling now. He could tell she was relieved, glad to have gotten off the subject of his father so easily. "Here," she said, "just a quart of skim. I hate to have to buy it at Jordan's. It's so much more expensive than the Giant.

"Be careful. Come right back. Be sure to turn on your light." Her warnings followed him down all three flights. He unlocked his bike from the rack in the hall and bumped it down the front stairs to the street.

He stopped before mounting his bike and took in a deep breath. It was cool but dry and clear. Someone was burning leaves. He loved the smell and the fact that someone out there in the dark was ignoring the ordinance against burning. I mean what did they expect you to do when all the streets were lined with giant oaks that buried the neighborhood with wave upon wave of crackling brown leaves.

"Hey, kid." A car had pulled to the opposite curb under the streetlight. Park pretended deafness. A man's head leaned out the window. "Excuse me!" he called. "Could you tell us how to get to the Presbyterian church?"

The car seemed full of heads, but the occupants couldn't be too dangerous, asking for directions to a church. The driver smiled at him, and the streetlight caught the glint of metal insignia on his shoulders.

"You passed the turn," Park said. "It's back that way. Your first right. Then it's just a couple of blocks. You can't miss it."

There was a sound of laughter from the car. "Hear that? Can't miss it."

"I don't think there'll be anybody there, though. Not this time of night."

"Well, they promised us somebody would be. They're letting a bunch of us sleep in the gym." Veterans, come for the dedication. Park felt a little jiggle of excitement. The driver was making a U-turn. "Thanks," he called.

Park wanted them to know. He needed to tell someone who would care. "Hey," he called. "My dad was in 'Nam."

The car had come around and was now beside him. "All right!" said the man in the front passenger seat.

The driver leaned forward to talk around his friend. "He bringing you down tomorrow?"

"He can't." Park said it solemnly, so they'd understand.

"I'm sorry, man," said the driver.

"Then we'll see *you*, right?"

"Yeah." Park smiled. "Yeah, maybe so." He jumped on his bike and started down the hill. The vets honked their horn as they pulled away from the curb. Park waved his hand high so they'd catch it in their rearview mirror.

By the time he got home again, he was determined. He would get his mother to talk to him—to tell him all about his father. Parkington Waddell Broughton, IV, deceased. On legal papers the *deceased* was always tacked on just like the Roman numeral.

"He is not really dead, you know. Morgana le Fay has cast a spell upon him and he lies, as though sleeping, these many years in a castle deep in the great forest where the sun never breaks through. But you, you have been chosen for this quest to find the dread castle and to wage battle against the evil enchantment. You, his only son. Yet the perils are unmeasured—" He shook off all thought of danger. He must go. For his father's sake and for the lady's.

Park took the stairs two at a time, brandishing the quart of skim like a battle-ax. He unlocked the apartment door and flung it open. "Mom!"

She was nowhere to be seen. For a second he panicked, just as when he was tiny and had lost her in a crowded mall. "Mom!"

"In here."

He followed her voice to the bedroom. She was sitting on the edge of her bed with her back to the door. The light was off.

Park switched it on. "What's the matter? Why are you sitting here in the dark?"

"Did you put the milk away?" Her words sounded muffled.

He put the carton in the refrigerator and then came back to her doorway. "Can I do anything for you?" He wanted to walk around and look her in the face, but something held him on the threshold.

"No. Thanks. I think I'll turn in early."

"Mom"—he spoke as gently as he could—"about my dad . . ."

"Oh, Pork," she said. "Please don't ask me to go back."

Go back where? "I just want to know—" He stopped. Just want to know what? Just everything. That was all. How should he begin?

In the apartment across the hall, Mr. Campanelli was yelling something to his deaf wife. Three flights below in the street, a horn sounded. If he just knew the right question, the one that would unlock all the others—

"Another time, all right?" She had turned, and her mouth was twisted into a kind of smile. "Do you want help with the couch?"

He shook his head. It was not yet eight o'clock, but he pulled the couch out anyway, got the covers from the closet shelf, and made his bed—or made it as well as he ever did without his mother supervising, giving lectures on the virtues of hospital corners and making sure the quilt was tucked in all across the bottom.

He even turned the TV on low, though he wasn't watching. He wasn't even dreaming of himself on his knees before King Arthur or rescuing a maiden from the jaws of a dragon.

He was lying on the couch replaying the scene with his mother. What should he have said? Right in the very beginning when he said he wanted to go to the ceremonies? What right did she have to decide for him? She decided everything. "Another time, all right?" What other time? It was long past time that he knew about his father. Park wanted to know how and why he had died—even when. Deceased: January 22, 1973. It seemed plain enough until you began to think about time zones. That would have been a different day in America, or had they figured it in when they set the date? He needed to know stupid little things like that.

Not to mention bigger things. For instance, if he, Park,

13

was Parkington Waddell Broughton the Fifth, then there had been not only a fourth (deceased), but a third, a second, a first. There was, or there had been, a family somewhere who valued that awful name so much that they kept giving it to boys who would hate it themselves and yet still grow up to insist on giving it to their own sons, even when it was far too long to fit in the blank space on a school form.

Parkington Waddell Broughton III might still be alive. Park shivered at the thought. He might have a grandfather somewhere with the same name he had. Why didn't Park know for sure? Wouldn't a man want to keep in touch with his own namesake?

Park put his hands behind his neck and stretched out his legs. The sofa bed was short, and he could almost get his toes to the end when he scrunched down and stretched out. He wasn't a kid anymore—his mother shouldn't treat him as she had tonight. He was growing up. She couldn't keep him cramped into her narrow life much longer. He would have to make her tell him about his father—about his father's family. But how? How could he stand to make her pretty face old and ugly with the remembering?

"Woman, the time has come." She shrank back from him into the shadows of the cave. "No," he said firmly. "Shrink not from me. The King has sent me to be your deliverer. Give me the knowledge that I seek, and I will break this enchantment that holds your kingdom in thrall. For if you will not—"

The woman began to weep softly. "How can I tell thee, noble sir, the word that will bring peril to your very life?"

"Tell me," he said, "though it slay me."

She turned to him, extending her palms in a gesture of surrender. "It is as thou willest. Listen. . . ."

But he did not hear. The woman was gone. He would never learn the secret he longed to uncover. Park got up and shut off the TV and then the light.

No. He sat up in bed. He would know. He would learn all about his father. He had to. No matter what she said.

HEART OF DARKNESS

·2·

As soon as his mother left for work, he ran to the little bureau in the living room where he kept his clothes and took a coffee can from the top drawer. He poured the contents onto the couch and pushed the nails, screws, buttons, and bottle caps to one side. Sixty-eight cents, forty-eight of it in pennies. If he could get the 7-Eleven to give him real money for the pennies, he could go downtown, even if he didn't have enough to ride back. What the hey. He could ask somebody for Metro money. Grown people hung around the stops doing that. Or he could walk. It couldn't be much more than five miles. He might even run into the guys from last night or someone else he knew. He was putting on his jacket when the phone rang. As soon as he answered it, he knew he should have just let it ring.

"Pork?" It was his mother. "You all right?" She was checking on him. She knew he might be thinking of going down on his own. She was making sure he wouldn't dare leave the stupid apartment. He mumbled the promise she demanded, then hung up. Without taking off his jacket, he switched on the TV and dropped down on the couch.

In the National Cathedral people were reading names of those who died in Vietnam—hour after hour they had been reading. They were long past the *B*'s, but he listened as long as the segment was on, hoping somehow that the reader would know he'd just tuned in and would read his father's name just for him. He strained to listen, but the announcer's voice soon covered over the reading, and when they again allowed the sound of names to swell up like music in the huge church, his father's name was not among them.

"I must find the Green Chapel, lest I be a coward and no true knight."

"Ah, sirrah, then your death be upon your own hands, for many a man has sought to go to that cursed place, but no man has yet returned."

Down the dark path rode Sir Gawain, into the valley of despair, for it was his sworn duty to go this day to the Green Chapel and offer himself to the Green Knight, who awaited him there. Even as he rode, he could hear the sound of the dreaded axe being sharpened upon the grindstone—

With all his dreaming, Park had never dared to dream much about his father. Perhaps he had been afraid to, but now he recognized the dull ache in his stomach as a longing.

He wanted more than anything at that moment to know the man whose name he carried.

He had seen only one picture of his father, and he had found that one day flipping through a book. He went now to the bookshelf and took down the volume of poems that hid the smiling, almost mischievous face. He searched the features for some echo of his own. It only made him sad. His own face was round and formless, the face of an overgrown baby. The face that smiled out at him was thin and strong. There was no resemblance Park could discover. The photo was black and white, so he couldn't even tell if the colors matched, but he was afraid they wouldn't. His own eyes were pale blue and his hair almost white, it was so light. The eyes in the picture looked black, and the hair was dark but straight. Park's hair was straight, too. Not like his mother's, which ruffled round her thin face like a baby doll's.

His father had a strong nose, straight as a movie star's, not short and pinched off like his own. And no glasses. Of course. People who wear glasses can't pilot bombers.

Park sighed and started to replace the picture, but his hunger drew his eyes to the pages between which he had found it. His mother read lots of books, but he had never seen her take this one from the living room shelf. In fact, the only books she read, besides the many she brought from the library, were the ones in the small case in her bedroom.

> If all the griefs I am to have
> Would only come today,
> I am so happy I believe
> They'd laugh and run away.

When had he ever felt that happy? He certainly couldn't imagine his mother feeling so happy. He read on.

If all the joys I am to have
Would only come today,
They could not be so big as this
That happens to me now.

Scrawled beside the word *today* in the second verse was a
date—*6/23/70*. Was that the day his parents got married?
Surely he ought to know his own parents' anniversary.

He looked down at the next poem. Maybe the hidden
secrets were all tucked into the pages of this book.

My life closed twice before its close—
It yet remains to see
If Immortality unveil
A third event to me
So huge, so hopeless to conceive
As these that twice befell.
Parting is all we know of heaven,
And all we need of hell.

He felt suddenly as though he had fallen into a dark hole,
far from the light. Which poem was the picture meant to
mark?

There was no date, no writing at all on the second poem,
but— Park carried it over to the lamp and switched on the
light. He raised his glasses and held the page close to his
face. Yes, the page was smudged, as though, as though— He
could see Randy crying over it, splotching the words. He had
seldom seen her cry, but looking at this page, he saw her as
clear as his own daydreams, her eyes red, her face puffy.

What was he to make of these two poems, the one right
on the heels of the other? One ringing with exuberant laughter, the other leaden with pain? And his father's picture
holding the place. It had to mean something—like the giant

sword growing out of the stone—but he did not have the strength or the magic power to pull it out.

He turned again to the flyleaf. *Broughton* sprawled in the corner in a large, comfortable hand. The book must have belonged to his father. His father must have written that date on page 314. But he had not smudged the opposite page with tears, Park was sure of that.

These books. What a stupid kid he was! These books must have belonged to his father. Why hadn't he thought of that before? These were the books that Randy never touched, and she loved books. And he—he had looked at their spines a million times. He'd even taken one or two of them from the case to see if there was something he'd want to read, but they had seemed shabby and boring. He'd never thought of them as a living link to his father. Only the book of poems— and that was because he'd found the picture of his father stuck inside—not because of the book itself.

Books tell you about the person who chose them. Of course. At school Mrs. Winslow, the librarian, often called him over to say "Here's a book I think you'd like," and she was nearly always right. She didn't make a thing of it in front of other people; still she knew what Park did or didn't like. He hated books about machines and computers. Even when he was in the second grade, he had hated dinosaurs and loved dragons. He hated information books almost as much as he hated sappy novels with kids moaning about their problems. There were enough problems in real life without having to take on someone else's phony ones.

No, Mrs. Winslow gave him dragons and castles and all the King Arthur tales she could find. She never criticized you for what you liked, either. She'd give Sheila Clark some idiot book called *Meet Mr. Atom* with her left hand while she was handing him *The Sword and the Circle* with her right. But the point was, Mrs. Winslow knew what you were like because of the books you liked. If he were to read the books in his father's bookcase, wouldn't he know at least as much about his father as Mrs. Winslow knew about him?

Park chose the largest, fattest book, so tall it had to sit spine-up in the low shelf. If he read it first, the rest would seem easy. He was rewarded at once. The first page of the book had an inscription: *Happy birthday to Park from Dad. August 4, 1960. You're old enough for Conrad now.* His grandfather.

He was trembling. His father's father. Randy didn't talk about relatives, even her own. Oh, occasionally she'd mention Mama, who was dead, and Daddy and his wife, whom she'd never gotten along with. On his father's side there was simply a blank wall. Nothing. Of course, Park knew his father must have had parents. Maybe even brothers and sisters. Randy had a stepsister. He'd seen her once. All he could remember was that she wore lots of green stuff smudged on her eyelids.

And here suddenly was his missing grandfather. He liked the handwriting. It was big and masculine-looking and reminded him of the sprawling *Broughton* written in the poetry book.

He turned to the title page. Conrad was the name of the author. The book had several long stories by him. The first was called "Youth," and at the top of the page was a man on the deck of what might have been a tug looking out at a sailing ship. Sea stories. When his father was— Well, how could he know how old, when he wasn't even sure when his father had been born? Anyhow, when he had been a boy, *his* father (Parkington Waddell Broughton, III) had given him sea stories. He wished for a fraction of a minute that they might have been about the Round Table, but only for

22

a fraction. He couldn't ask that his father be just like himself, and at least these were going to be adventure stories.

Before he began to read, he made a vow. With his hand on his father's picture, lying on the open page of poems, he swore to read the books on his father's shelf, and then, when he had earned the right, to visit the memorial and look for his father's name.

That was November. All of December and part of January were haunted by Conrad's strange stories. Park could only read them when his mother was gone. He was afraid she'd catch him with his father's book, reading these dark, powerful tales that pulled him into a deep forest where he could not see his way. But he had to keep reading, not to understand the stories themselves, which were really beyond his understanding, but to seek for the path through the forest to the enchanted place where his father and, perhaps, his grandfather were being held in thrall.

He read *The Heart of Darkness* and remembered in a cold sweat the winter day a couple of years before when his mother had plopped him into the car and driven all the way to the coast of Delaware without speaking a word to him. When they got at last to Bethany Beach, there were acres of empty parking lots with hardly a car, much less another human being in sight. The gulls circled and swooped, crying out in cold, hungry squawks. His mother had taken his hand as though he were five and headed for the oceanfront. The cold salt air stung his nostrils, and his sneakers sank into the damp sand so that he had to struggle to keep up as she jerked him along, not looking at him, just looking at the angry white foam roaring into the land. There was a small boat bouncing about on the waves. Park had been afraid for it. He wanted to say so, but he couldn't speak. Something in his mother's face forbade it. She turned, finally, and went back to the car, startling a flock of gulls that had found a beached fish and were fighting over it.

She never spoke until they were almost back to Washington. She pulled into a McDonald's and asked if he was hungry. When he nodded, she took him inside and ordered a hamburger and shake for him and coffee for herself. He wanted fries—she always got him fries—but he wasn't able to say so. Her face was white and hard as the side of the drink machine, and her hand shook as she lifted her cup and hid behind the Styrofoam.

The next day she was herself again. They never talked about that trip to the beach, and they had never gone back.

Conrad, Park thought, was something like that day. There was so much he couldn't understand, so much that Conrad was refusing to tell him, and yet the power of the story pounded away inside him like a grief too deep for words— like the cry of a hungry gull in a winter sky.

Since that day, he'd had to look at his mother differently. She was younger than many of the mothers of his schoolmates. She was thin as a magazine model, with blonde hair curling softly about her face. Her eyes were a clear blue, and her skin was pale and smooth except for a mole under the outside corner of her left eye. If you didn't know her, you'd see her as a pretty blonde. But from time to time he would get a glimpse of something hidden deep inside her—something that frightened him.

She never hit him. She hardly ever yelled. No one could say she wasn't a good mother. There were many days, indeed most days, when she was kind and fun to be with. But behind her bantering was this coldness, this darkness, this heart of darkness that he couldn't fathom. It had to do with his father;

he was sure now of that. But his father had been dead ten years. How long was a person supposed to grieve?

Other people lost husbands and got over it. Greg Henning's father walked out on them. His mother bawled three or four months, then washed her face and got on with life. In September she got married again, and Greg said she was as happy as a teenybopper. Park's father had been dead ten years, and Randy never even had a date. She was lots better looking than Greg's mother—smarter, too. Greg's mother was cotton candy, pink fluff down to her paper core. There was nothing deep inside to comfort or to scare you.

In the laundromat one Saturday last summer, Park saw a man watching his mother's trim little bottom as she leaned over the dryer. The man was grinning in a friendly way—a little fresh, maybe, but not so you'd mind it. He was still smiling when Randy straightened up and turned around. The man opened his mouth. He was about to say something, try to get her into a conversation, but one look at Randy's face and he stopped cold and began to fold his underwear as though it were the most important job in the world.

She loved Park. He knew that. When he was little, she had read to him. He would crawl up on her bed and sit as close to her as he could, smelling her fresh, perfumed soap smell, touching when he could her pale arm, the hairs so blonde they were nearly invisible. He loved to blow on them and make her giggle in protest. She was not a giggler as a rule.

In her soft voice which still held a slight trace of her native Texas, she read him nursery rhymes and fairy tales and hundreds of picture books that they brought home every Saturday from the library. Sometimes the stories were funny, and they would laugh together. Once when she was reading

Winnie-the-Pooh—it was the story about Piglet and the Heffalump—she got hysterical laughing at what was going to happen next and couldn't keep reading. "Mom, Mom," he had cried, jerking at the sleeve of her bathrobe, "what's so funny?" And she struggled to tell him what her eye had traveled ahead to, but when she tried to speak, the words came out in little shrieks and squeaks and he couldn't understand, so there was nothing for him to do but fall out laughing himself.

Now that he read well, she didn't read to him anymore. He missed it more than he could say.

Between November and February, Park read more than he had in all his life put together. When his mother was asleep or at work, he would steal a book from the living room shelf. He couldn't read Conrad all in one gulp. Between those dense, heavy stories, he zipped through detective novels and took reluctant bites out of weird modern stories that made you feel you ought to tell the characters to grow up and stop whining. It bothered him that his father had read such books. His father had been a warrior, not a whiner.

Always he went back to Conrad. Such heaviness on every page! Sometimes he would stop and escape to the book of poetry—to its clean, light lines with great white open spaces for breathing. He'd just sit there, without reading, just looking at the space as a way of resting from all the darkness.

February came. Park had at least sampled every book on those three narrow shelves. He waited until his mother was put on weekends, and then on the first Saturday, after she left for work, he got out the Metro map and figured out the best route to the memorial. He would go this time even if she tried to stop him. His vow of servitude was fulfilled. He was ready to take up his quest.

He made himself a peanut butter and jelly sandwich.

There wasn't much choice when Randy worked weekends. He put on his ski jacket and headed for the Metro stop. The sun was high and warm. It was a false spring day. Only when the wind came up and blew cold on his ears and cheeks did he remember that it was still winter.

On Saturdays there were fewer trains, so he stood inside the platform shelter to keep out of the wind, and held his face up toward the sun. He shut his eyes against the brightness and felt a tiny flip of excitement inside his chest. Today I'm going to meet my father, it said. He could see him coming toward him, tall and straight in the blue uniform with silver wings above the left pocket. The hat was at a tilt, but the airman took it off and held it in his hand, spreading his arms wide and stooping a little, waiting for Park to come running like a tiny child—

That was not true. His father was dead.

THE BLACK STONE

· 3 ·

He wished he'd worn a cap. His mother was always after him to wear something on his head, which made it hard for him simply to go to the closet, take a cap off the hook, and put it on. Today she was at work and wouldn't have known whether he wore one, but the habit of resisting was too strong. It hadn't occurred to him that in the empty sweep between the Washington Monument and the Lincoln Memorial he would have liked to have something to keep the wind from making his ears ache and throb. The metal frames of his glasses cut icily into both sides of his head.

His eyes hurt, too, from straining to find what he had

come to see. It was nowhere. The guy at the Metro had told him it was beyond the Washington Monument, but there was nothing to be seen but a grassy expanse of parkland. There were no park police, hardly any people around at all. And he was shy about asking those few he saw. How stupid not to know where the Vietnam memorial was. The papers had been full of it last fall. Everyone knew where it was, except him.

At last he saw the sign, small and not very high, that pointed in the same direction he was headed. And then, without warning, he was there. A sidewalk led him beside a black stone wall that grew down into the earth, getting taller as he walked slowly toward the lowest point, and then gradually diminishing again as the path went up—like a beautifully polished giant boomerang cutting into the surface of the lawn—and covered with names etched exquisitely into the ebony face of the rock.

There were other people on the walk, standing before panels of the shining stone, searching the infinite lines of names and, finding one, fingering the contours of the letters. Park, too, felt the urge to reach out and feel the surface of the stone, but he clenched his fist in his pocket. The first name he touched must be his father's.

And when they were all gathered in the great hall at Camelot to celebrate the feast of Pentecost, suddenly the mighty doors were opened and a light shone brighter than seven suns. And there entered into the hall, borne by an unseen arm, the Holy Grail, draped in a cloth of blinding white. Then the hall was filled with the odors of meats and wines and they all ate and were filled from the bounty of the Holy Vessel, and no man knew whence it came nor whither it had departed. The knight sat in silence, bedazzled by the vision, and swelling up in his heart was the command, "Follow. Follow and find."

But how was he to find his father's name? The names went on and on; there were thousands of them. He would never find just one.

"Are you looking for someone special?" He turned to see a middle-aged woman in a beige felt hat and tweed overcoat. "It's all right," she said, smiling. "That's what I'm here for, to help." She led him back to the top of the walk, where there was a line of books like the metropolitan area telephone books. She opened one. "What name were you looking for?" she asked gently.

He cleared his throat. "Parkington Waddell Broughton the Fourth," he said.

She searched the book and then put her gloved finger on a place. "Panel 1 W," she said, "line 119."

He stood there, not certain what she meant. "It's this way," she said with her elegant, gentle smile, and led him down to where the black granite was tallest.

She showed him how to count by the marks at the end of every tenth line and then left him to count down for himself, as though she knew he wouldn't want a stranger with him when he first saw it. And there it was: PARKINGTON W. BROUGHTON IV.

He reached out, grateful that on that tall stone the name he needed could be reached, and lightly traced the letters of his father's name. The stone felt warm from the winter sun. It wasn't like a gravestone at all. It was like something alive and lovely. He could see his own hand reflected across his father's name. Tears started in his eyes, surprising him, be-

31

cause he felt so happy to be here, so close to actually touching that handsome man in his jaunty cap with the tie of
his uniform loose and the neck unbuttoned.

He wished he had brought something to leave. Other
people had left flowers or a single carnation stuck into the
seam of the stone beside a name. There were medals and
campaign ribbons at the foot of some of the panels and,
further to one end, a teddy bear, propped against the granite.
But none of it seemed trashy or out of place, any more than the
silent people who stood there, touching names and weeping.

Riding home on the Metro, he wondered about many
things. Who the guide had been—someone's mother, perhaps. His own mother—had she ever been to the memorial?
Without telling him, just to run her fingers across the warm
stone? He could hardly believe that she had not gone, but if
she had, wouldn't it have comforted her, the way it had
comforted him? Wouldn't she have come home and told him
and then taken him so that they could touch the name together? He so wanted now to tell her, to take her. He wanted
to see her pale face mirrored in the shining granite. He
wanted to see her thin fingers take strength from the crevices
that formed his father's name.

They needed him. Dead or not. They couldn't keep living
with the pretense that he had never been. They needed the
life flowing from his memory—even if the memories were
sad. Wasn't sad better than no feeling at all? Wasn't the
anger of that day at Bethany Beach better than endless frozen
years?

If she didn't need him, or didn't think she did, Park must
tell her that she had no right to choose for them both. He
needed his father.

"Where have you been?"

She had beaten him home. Park took off his jacket and hung it carefully in the closet instead of throwing it in the direction of the couch as he more often did.

"Pork? Where have you been?" she called again from the kitchen. "I was worried. You didn't leave a note."

He went to the kitchen door. Randy's pale face was flushed from the heat of the stove. She cocked her head and gave a shy half smile.

"I went," he started, not wanting to pain her, but pushing the words out all the same. His own need was greater than the need not to cause her pain. "I went to see the memorial." Her eyes clouded. "The Vietnam memorial. I found his name."

She turned her back on him, as though busying herself with the supper. The Saturday casserole was already smelling up the apartment with onion and noodles and tomato sauce and hamburger. She began to tear lettuce. "How could you find it?" she asked at last. "There must be thousands of names."

"Fifty thousand," he said. "More than." She didn't turn around, but he went on, sure of her attention. "They have a book, like a map, an index. A woman showed me."

"Oh."

"You've never been?"

"Me? No."

"It's beautiful," he said. "And it made me know—" How could he explain? If he told her that after the vision, all the knights had gone in quest of the Grail, would she understand? No, he was sure she wouldn't. "It made me feel— it made me think—" She was silent. She was not going to help him, so he blurted it out like a three-year-old: "I gotta know him."

33

"He's dead."

"I gotta know about him."

She turned toward him then. "Oh, Pork," she said. "Please—you don't know what you're asking."

"I read his books," Park said, jerking his head back toward the bookcase in the other room. "Most of them. And the poems." She stood unmoving, unblinking. "Other people have fathers every day. Can't I have a little piece of mine?"

"He died years ago."

"Then tell me about him," he begged her stiff body. "Please, Mom, I really need to know."

"I can't," she said, turning her back to him again, her body sagging a little, growing weaker as he watched. "Please understand, I can't, but—"

"Yeah?"

"He has—he had a family—" She let out a sigh as loud as her words. "Maybe it's time—"

He went to her then and put his arms around her and rested his chin on her shoulder. Her back stiffened again, resisting his embrace.

"Summer," she said, slipping lightly away from him. "Maybe you can go visit them in the summer. I'll have to write. I don't know what they'll say. They never"—she gave a choked little laugh—"they never really approved of me. Poor little West Texas white trash coming into their family." She laughed again. "Generals and colonels and gentlemen Virginia farmers right back to the time of old George himself."

Park guessed she meant Washington, but he wasn't going to interrupt her to ask. Not now.

"It's been years since I've seen them, at least two years since I've heard anything—" She stopped herself and jammed a salad bowl into his hands. "You'll have to be patient—"

34

"Sure," he said, putting the salad on the dinette table. "I can wait. It's okay."

"It'll have to be," she said wearily. "Don't get your hopes up too much. A lot has happened since— They may not be thrilled, you know."

He didn't know. Of course they'd want to see him. He was the Fifth. He belonged in the family line.

THE HIRED MAN

· 4 ·

"Grandsire!"

The old man looked up at the word. He was sitting on a circular bench under a spreading oak two hundred years old—planted by the first king of this noble line who, when he tended that tiny sapling, could never have dreamed of the scene taking place today.

Leaning heavily on his staff, the old king rose slowly. "My child," he said, his voice quavering with emotion. "Can it really be? Thou at last returned from thy quest?"

The young knight ran forward then, and when he got to where the old man stood, he stretched out his hand, but his elder ignored it, dropping his staff and throwing both arms around the strong young shoulders. "God is good," he said, the words choked with unshed tears—

"How old is my grandfather?" Park put down his cereal spoon.

"I haven't written them yet," Randy said. "He may be dead."

Standing by the grave in the ancient chapel, the youth could not hold back the tears, as unmanly as some might think them. Too late. Too late. Oh, that he had come in time—

No. Park wasn't going to let his grandfather die without seeing him. Quickly he revised the picture in his head. Now the man waiting at the oak tree was tall and straight with a sword bound at his waist. "How old would he be now?"

"The Colonel? I don't know. I'm not sure I ever knew. His hair was white the first time I saw him, but he had a young face—" Pain crossed her own. He looked like my father, Park thought. She's remembering the resemblance. She tossed her head. "He could have been any age." And then, looking at Park, "You mustn't ask so many questions when you go, *if* you go. People don't like kids who are always asking questions. Besides, it makes you seem even younger than you are. Three-year-olds are expected to ask questions all the time, not eleven-year-olds."

It wasn't fair. He shoved his glasses back on the bridge of his nose. "I only asked you how old—"

She let out a sharp *foof* of a sigh. "I don't really know. He was in the war, if that helps."

Park opened his mouth to ask which war, checked himself, and turned the question into a statement. "World War II."

She nodded. "Although you could pick a war, any war, and you'd have a Broughton in it. The Broughtons have always been crazy about war." She spoke so bitterly that he picked up the cereal box and began reading the contents of the package.

She never told Park she had written. Then one day toward the end of May, when he took the mail from the box in the downstairs hallway, there was a letter with BROUGHTON printed in a small, neat hand in the upper left corner of the envelope and a rural route address in Strathaven, Virginia.

He got out the atlas and searched, finally flipping to the index to find the letter and number. He hated looking things up in indexes, but he wasn't sure how much time he'd have before his mother got home. She didn't usually get home before six, and then, just when you'd least expect it, she'd work half day instead of whole and there she'd be. You ought to be able to count on when your mother would or would not be home. She always demanded to know his exact schedule, which was hard, as he never knew when he'd be going over to Greg's house or wanting to go up to the 7-Eleven or drop by the library or just hang around the end of Walnut Street across from the library and throw a football around or something. If he didn't leave a note—when, where, why, and with whom—she would hit the ceiling. (Randy always said "whom" to show she'd been to college.)

He found Strathaven down toward the southwest corner of Virginia. Durn. He'd hoped it would be in the northeast— even on the Metro line, so he could hop over one Saturday and scout it out. But it was almost as far away from D.C. as it could be and still be in Virginia.

He picked up the envelope and held it up in front of the window. He could see writing but, with the sheets folded against each other, it was unreadable. He tried to calculate how long the letter might be. Long was good, short bad, as he figured it. Short, they'd be saying they didn't want to see him; long, they were trying to reestablish contact, tell her the family news and ask all about him. Short, forget you.

Dear Randy—Dear Mrs. Broughton—Salutations to our beloved sister— How could he imagine a letter from relatives he'd never seen, never even known existed until a few months ago? *What a joy it was—* Yes, yes. *What a joy it was to hear from you again after all these years and to know that you and the lad are both well. Do come! Come at once! Both of you! No, no! We cannot wait. We will come to you—*

To this apartment? What would they think? Two steps up from a slum? A family that served in the army with George Washington?

"He said it would be all right for you to come." That was all Randy reported to him of the letter. She didn't even explain who "he" was, but it had to be his grandfather, didn't it? Park felt sure it was. She must have destroyed the letter because, hunt as he might, he never found it among her things.

The man who met him at the Greyhound was short and lean, muscled, with a dark red face, hands, and neck. His eyes were steely gray and his hair dark. The hired man, Park decided. He had hoped his grandfather would come himself, but Broughtons probably didn't come to bus stations. They sent one of the men to pick up guests. But then they probably didn't have guests who could only afford to ride the bus.

Park straightened. He wanted the hired man to realize

40

at once that he was his father's son. He needn't have worried. The man had picked him out immediately as he came down the steps off the bus. He'd come forward with a shy smile and stuck out his hand. "Frank," he'd said.

Were you supposed to shake hands with the help? Park hesitated long enough for the man to grin and drop his hand. "Your bag underneath?" he asked.

Park blushed and nodded. The man stuck out his hand again. This time Park grabbed it and shook it with both his own. He mustn't seem stuck-up to the man, even though he was Parkington the Fifth. The man smiled again. "I was needing your stub—your baggage check."

"Oh," said Park, "oh," and fumbled through his windbreaker pockets and then three pants pockets before he pulled the check from the back one, a bit worse for wear, having been sat on all the way from Washington.

The man called Frank helped the driver extract Park's bag from the belly of the bus and then nodded for Park to follow him. The bag suddenly seemed very small and shabby. He probably should have carried it on board instead of letting Randy check it. He hoped the hired man didn't think of that.

Grandfather had not seen fit to send the Lincoln. Frank had driven to town in a Toyota pickup. He flung the bag up into the back as though it weighed nothing, opened the cab door, and swung up into the driver's seat. "It's not locked," he called out the passenger window to Park, who still stood watching on the sidewalk.

Once more Park blushed and hurried to climb up beside Frank in the cab. "I probably should have brought the car," Frank was now confessing. "I thought a boy might like—well, to tell the truth, I guess I'd rather drive this."

Park nodded to show that he had no hard feelings. He wouldn't even mention the incident to Grandfather.

"I understand Frank went to meet you in the pickup. He knows better. On your first visit, too."

"No matter, sir. He meant no harm. Really. It was fine."

"You just can't get good help these days."

"It was fine. Truly, it was. Don't reprimand him."

A sigh. "As you say, my lad."

"So what do they call you?"

"What?"

"What do they call you?"

Park straightened his glasses and then his shoulders. "Parkington Waddell Broughton the Fifth."

The man laughed softly. "I know the name," he said. "But no one's ever called by it, are they?"

"Park," Park said decisively. After all, that's what he went by at school. His mother wasn't here to argue.

"Just like your dad."

"Yeah," Park said. The man sitting beside him had known his father. He forced his voice to remain steady. "You been with the Broughtons a long time?"

The man glanced over at him. "All my life," he said. And then, "Randy didn't tell you much about us, I take it."

Park bit his lip. "No."

"I'm your Uncle Frank—your dad's kid brother."

"I didn't know." Park's voice went squeaky in embarrassment. "Nobody told me."

"It's all right. How could you know?"

"But I—I thought you were—well, somebody that worked for my grandfather."

"Well," said Frank, laughing, "I am that."

"How—how is—how is he?"

"She didn't tell you that either?" Frank glanced at him. "No. Well, I guess she couldn't really know. He's not in very good shape."

"Oh."

"About two years ago, he had another stroke. I—we thought he might go then. I wrote Randy. In case—but she didn't—"

"No." He didn't even try to hide his feelings, his disappointment. *Another* stroke? He had pictured his grandfather as a noble, white-haired warrior. He couldn't put him into a hospital bed.

"I told him you were coming." Frank was speaking very carefully. "I'm afraid it upset him. He gets, well, agitated. We'll just have to see how it goes."

Did that mean he might not even meet Park the Third? He was only to be here for two weeks. Suppose the old man stayed agitated all that time? Surely Frank wasn't going to keep him from meeting his grandfather altogether? Why had he said it was all right for Park to come if the old man was too sick even to see him?

"How old is he?" Park asked, promising himself not to ask another question, but he had needed the answer to this one for months.

"Let's see. Nineteen twenty-one. He must be sixty-three."

"That's not old!" It wasn't fair. Mr. Campanelli was seventy-five, and he jogged two miles every morning.

"No," Frank said. "It shouldn't be."

He had used up his one question, and the answer had been all wrong. He had a young grandfather who was worse than an old man. Park needed to ask if he was paralyzed all over. Wasn't a stroke the thing that made old people para-

43

lyzed? Could he walk? Did his brain work right? Would he recognize Park? Know who he was? If he could, if he could know that Park's son had come home at last, wouldn't it make him better? Wouldn't he be glad to see his long-lost grandson?

I told him you were coming. I'm afraid it upset him.

Why should it upset him? Maybe Frank couldn't tell whether the old man was upset or happy. They rode in silence the rest of the way. Disappointment lodged in Park's throat like a balled-up fist. They had turned off the main road leading from town onto a winding two-lane country road. It was a clear day in late June, not nearly so humid as Washington had been when he left this morning. In Richmond, waiting for the connecting bus, he'd eaten the bologna sandwich his mother had made him. She'd given him fifty cents to buy a soda, but he'd lost it in the drink machine. He tried to ask the woman at the lunch counter for a refund, but she just shrugged the shoulders of her soiled uniform. Refunds weren't her responsibility.

Randy had given him ten one-dollar bills for emergency, but he'd been so afraid he'd lose them that he'd tucked them, with his return ticket, into the side pocket inside his suitcase, and then Randy had checked the bag straight through to Strathaven.

Now, leaning his head out the window of the pickup, he thought he would die of thirst. Or humiliation. Or disappointment. The wind whipped through his hair—the hair that he had so carefully combed, peering into the dirty little mirror in the lavatory in the back of the Greyhound while it bounced him from side to side as it thundered down the interstate.

The pickup was slowing down. Park turned to see Frank

throw the gears into neutral, pull on the emergency, and hop out to open a long metal gate. He jumped back in, drove through, and hopped out again to close the gate. He could have asked me to open and close the gate, Park thought. Why didn't he ask me? Does he think I'm nothing? Then he looked up and saw the house.

RETURN OF THE
YOUNG MASTER

·5·

It was a white clapboard house—enormous, three stories, wrapped about, as far as he could see, with double-decker porches. On the side facing the drive there was a little roofed cupola with arched windows, ruffled with snowball bushes at least five feet high. It was as near to a castle as one might find in Virginia.

With a fanfare of trumpets and a creaking of chains, the giant drawbridge was lowered. As they entered the courtyard, servants scurried out of the many arched doors and lined themselves according to station. The men in tunics of green and brown, the women in blues and amber. *What color exactly was amber?* A murmur rustled through the line like wind through poplars. "The young lord. The young lord has returned." They bowed, not obsequiously, but with a fitting dignity and right true welcome—

Frank parked the pickup under an elm near the picket fence. "Welcome," he said.

Park climbed out of the cab. He meant to get his own suitcase, so his uncle wouldn't think he was some spoiled, stupid brat, but Frank had already swung it over the side and was opening the small white gate, which was weighted so that it swung closed after them. A large brown and black dog with shaggy hair and a sweeping tail came loping around the end of the porch and, tongue lolling happily out of the side of its mouth, offered its head to be patted by Frank.

"This is Jupe," Frank said, scratching the dog on his head and under his collar. Park wondered if he should try to pet the animal and decided not. He seemed too much Frank's. Suppose, just when Park was trying to look cool, the stupid dog took a hunk out of his hand? Jupe glanced at Park, as though mildly curious as to who he might be, but didn't make any move to investigate him. At least the mutt didn't growl. Park liked dogs okay, or to be precise, he'd always thought he'd like them, given a chance. Actually, the only dog he'd ever been around much was Greg Henning's mother's poodle, who didn't let anyone touch its snooty little body except Greg's mother—not even her new husband, much to the man's annoyance and Greg's amusement.

Jupe accompanied them up the walk, sticking close to Frank's side, the side away from Park. When they got to the edge of the porch, the dog stopped, as though he knew he had reached a boundary, and watched worshipfully, his tail flicking rhythmically, as Frank led Park down the long porch to the front door of the farmhouse.

"Sada?" Frank called as they stepped into the hallway, which was dim and cool. A woman of fifty or so, a little plump with frizzy gray hair, came toward them down the dark hall.

"This is young Park," Frank said. Park liked the sound of it—almost *young lord,* now wasn't it? "Park, this is Mrs. Davenport, who takes care of things here."

Davenport fit. The woman was dumpy and overstuffed, and she wore a loose housedress with large yellow and blue roses splashed across it. Park stuck out his hand.

The woman smiled and, jutting her face out toward him, said, "So—this is our little man."

Park's hand jerked back to his side, but the woman didn't seem to notice.

"Our patient's not too happy this afternoon," she said primly to Frank.

Frank nodded. "I'll stop by and see him after I get the boy settled in. Where did you plan to put him?"

"I made up the right front room. Cleaned it thoroughly yesterday, though you'd never know." She sighed. "These old houses, you might as well not try." She leaned toward Park, as if she were going to let him in on a secret. "Dust," she said. "A never-ending battle. I fight. Oh, I fight, but who would ever—"

Frank was doing his best to smile politely, but as she went on, he was moving ever so steadily past her toward the stairs. Park stuck close behind.

"Can I count on you for supper tonight, then, Mr. Frank?" She raised her voice, because Frank had rounded the bottom of the stairs and started up.

Frank didn't answer, but it didn't seem to matter. She had turned to go back into the kitchen. Park followed him up the long staircase that began at the far end of the hall. At the top Frank turned right, opened a door, and nodded Park in. It was a huge room. Most of Park's apartment would have fit inside it. The ceilings were twelve, fifteen feet high and, even with two double beds, there was still enough room to skateboard around. There were windows on two sides—large windows looking out on the upper porch. There was a fireplace, blocked by a little iron stove whose black pipe disappeared into the chimney. Near the stove was a marble-top washstand with a white porcelain washbowl on it that was larger than the sink in his mother's kitchen, and a tall, fat water pitcher, also white. In the corner stood a huge piece of furniture with mirrored doors. There were dust balls between its legs.

Frank saw him staring. "We haven't done much to modernize this old place," he said, whether proudly or apologetically, Park couldn't be sure. "The bathroom is all the way downstairs and at the back. I'll show you now, if you like."

He followed Frank down the stairs. At the bottom there was a closed door immediately to the right and another closed door across the hall to the left. Frank opened the door on the right. It led into a tiny, dark hall, off which was a large bathroom with a tub up on clawed feet, a tiny sink—smaller than the washbasin in the upstairs room—and a toilet.

"Well," said Frank. "I'll leave you to it. I need to get back to work. Mrs. Davenport will be here"—he smiled a little, as if asking Park not to mind—"if you need anything." He hesitated. "My house is the little one on the other side of the vegetable garden, but—oh, you'll see us around."

Park wanted to ask who "us" might be and which room his grandfather was in and whether there was anyone else beside him and the doofy Mrs. Davenport in this big house, but he didn't want Frank to think he was a kid asking too many questions. He would have to be patient. Frank was smiling shyly at him, trying to get away.

"Thank you," Park said to him.

"Hope everything will be okay for you," Frank said, as though afraid it wouldn't be.

It was the middle of the afternoon. Park went back up to the big front room and found a place to hang his clothes behind one of the huge doors of the wardrobe. There was no closet or bureau, but behind the other door there were drawers. Several were filled with linen and blankets and smelled strongly of mothballs. One had been emptied for him, so he put away his T-shirts and underwear and socks and tried to decide where to put his toothbrush. You couldn't spit in a china basin, could you? Should he carry his toothbrush up and down every time he needed to brush his stupid teeth? Should he leave it downstairs? You couldn't ask questions like that. You ought to know the right thing to do. He'd have to figure it out later. For now he put it back into his suitcase and shoved that under one of the high beds.

He was settled. It had taken him, even with hunting and deciding, about ten minutes. It was still the middle of the afternoon. Now what?

He went to the front window and looked out. Across the yard, beyond the picket fence, was a huge garden. The corn was almost as tall as he was, the garden itself larger than the park beside the library. He angled himself to look as far to the left as possible, and, yes, there was the small white house that must be Frank's. He wondered why Frank would live in a tiny, newish house when there was so much room in this one. It was as though Frank really was the hired man, living in the hired man's house.

"The castle is yours."

"But, Uncle, it will be years before—"

"It matters not. This is your inheritance. You are the first son of the first son."

"But you are the one who has labored to make the land what it is."

"I was honored to keep it in trust for the day of your coming. I knew you would return."

It didn't fit. Even knowing Frank less than an hour, Park found it hard to believe that his uncle had been waiting breathlessly for the return of the true heir. Maybe, in fact, Frank hated him. After all, if he hadn't shown up, everything would have belonged to Frank. Now, even if his uncle didn't have to actually turn over everything to the first son of the first son, wouldn't the law at least make him share it with Park? He conjured up Frank's deeply tanned face. He searched it for signs of resentment, but found none. The eyes were gentle.

If he hates me, I would feel it, Park reasoned. It's more like he's worried—maybe for me—maybe for someone else. He didn't ask me any questions about myself or Randy. He wasn't trying to figure out what I was up to, coming here. On the other hand, he didn't try to catch me up on what's going on here. Maybe he thinks if he ignores me, I'll go away.

Park left the room quickly, closing the door sharply behind him. As he ran down the stairs, Mrs. Davenport materialized at the foot, her finger on her lips. "Our patient is resting," she said.

Park nodded, ducking his head to hide his chagrin. "Is it all right if I go outdoors?" he whispered.

She smiled her sugar-frosting smile. "Now don't do anything I wouldn't," she said and winked. For a minute he was afraid she might pat him on the head, but she didn't.

Park went through the back hall, closing the doors carefully behind him, and onto a large screened-in back porch crowded with buckets and cabinets and boots and farm gear of all sorts and sizes, most of it looking as though it hadn't been touched in years. He crossed the porch and stepped out into the backyard. It was still hot and muggy outside the house. Jupe wandered over, sniffed, then went back to lie in front of a doghouse under the shade of a huge maple.

The back gate of the picket fence swung on the same kind of metal weight and chain that the front did. Park went out, eyeing the dog to see whether or not he would make a dash for the open gate. Jupe lifted his head and gave Park a bored glance, then laid his nose down between his paws and shut his eyes. How did you make friends with a dog? It was going to be a long two weeks.

Down the hill he went, past chicken houses that seemed to swell with the clucking. He had just glanced up, hardly taken his eyes off his stupid feet when, alerted by the sharp smell, he looked down to see his right foot in the middle of a large, wet pile left by a cow or a horse or some such big animal. He felt sick to his stomach as he pulled a sort of greenish sneaker out. He turned his foot and swiped the sides and bottom on a patch of weeds and went on down the hill past a barn and a smaller shed with a trough in front. It seemed to be the pigsty, for he could see pigs further down the slope rooting in the mud beside a large, willow-lined pond.

He followed the winding dirt-and-gravel road past sheds of old machinery, climbed a rail gate, and walked on to the bottom of the hill to a tiny wooden house, out of which leaked a stream that fed the pond. He lifted a rusty latch and pushed open the door. It was dark inside. Even before his eyes adjusted to the darkness, he could hear the music of the spring and smell the pure fragrance of the water. It was flowing through a small metal pipe into a concrete trough. On a wooden ledge above the trough was a half coconut shell. He held the shell below the pipe and let it fill and then lifted it to his mouth. Never in his life had he tasted anything just like that water. It was as though he had never known before what water was. The clean, sweet taste was mixed faintly with the dry, grassy flavor of the shell. He drank it down. The water was so cold it hurt his chest.

Park sat on the edge of the trough, his feet on the flagstone floor of the springhouse. If I can come here every day, he thought, if I can come here, I will get through the weeks.

He got up and closed the door. A delicious quiet flowed through his body. Kneeling upon the cold stones, he took off his helmet and laid it before the altar. Watch and pray. If he kept faithful vigil, then at dawn he could appear before the High King and receive the sword upon his shoulder and become a knight of the realm, and, as deed of valor followed upon deed, perhaps see his name glowing upon a place at the Round Table itself. But until that day, would the fair lady who held his heart in her lily-white hands wait for him? He dared not a word until he had won her favor with acts of chivalry. No, he must not think of the lady. He must fix his mind this night upon the Grail. This night was for contemplation of the holy. The chalice began to glow with an unearthly light. Surely, a vision was being granted him, a sign—

"What you doing here?"

Park jumped up. In the doorway stood a girl, black, straight hair falling in dishevelment across a narrow brown face, a red baseball cap riding the back of her head like a sailboat. The hands at the end of her thin arms pressed against the doorjamb at shoulder height. She wore faded jeans and a once-white T-shirt.

"What you doing here?" she asked again.

He opened his mouth, but nothing came out.

"Mine," she said. "My place."

CHALLENGE FROM
A STRANGER

·6·

"Come out where I see you," she ordered, stepping aside, confident that he would obey. He did, blinking in the bright sunshine. "I never see you," she said. "What you name?"

"I'm Pork," he said humbly, although he towered over her.

"That pig!" she said contemptuously, making him realize too late that he had given her his baby name.

The girl was Indian or Chinese or something foreign. She certainly wasn't a Broughton, whatever she was.

She was staring him up and down, as though he were a horse for sale at an auction. "How old?"

Why don't you count my blinking teeth? he wanted to

say, but he controlled himself. She disliked him enough already. "Twelve," he said. Well, he would be in the fall. It was close enough, and he needed an edge. There was no telling how old she might be. She didn't offer her age. Park smiled to himself. If she wasn't saying, it was because she was younger and didn't want to admit it. Anyhow, he was at least a foot taller.

"You fat," she said, propping a small hand on her hip.

"I am not. I'm—I'm well built for my age."

She snickered. "Pork, Pork, fat pork pig," she sang, her eyes narrowing to a dare.

Who did she think she was? "Park!" he said. "Park!"

"Bark! Bark! Like dog. Oink! Oink! Like pig." She pinched her tiny nose between her thumb and forefinger. "Stink like pig, too."

He was so furious he couldn't speak. He whirled around and started up the hill at a fast clip, only to put his remaining clean shoe into a huge, gloopy pile. He could hear her laughing as he pulled out his sneakered foot and tried again to wipe the worst of the mess off on a rock and then on a bit of grass. He wouldn't give her the satisfaction of turning around. In his mind he pictured her rolling on the ground in front of the springhouse, hysterical with glee.

He marched on up the hill. Should he climb the gate or open it? He was sure there was a right way to do it, and whichever he chose would prove to be the wrong one. He decided on opening the gate, which seemed safer than hefting his bottom up across the rails with her watching from below. The latch consisted of a piece of wire bent and bound into an oval and looped over a fence post. He jerked off the wire, and the long wooden gate swung past, nearly knocking him over and banging heavily against the shed that sided the road.

He raced over to bring it back, but, of course, she had seen. Out of the side of his eye he could see her standing, feet apart, both hands on narrow hips, and he could hear her laughing. He held on tightly to the heavy gate, working his way awkwardly around to the uphill side, trying hard not to look at her while he pulled it shut and reattached the wire hoop.

He glanced at his watch. It was only four thirty. He dreaded the thought of going back to the cool tomb of a house to wait for supper. He walked as slowly as he could past what looked as if it should have been a horse barn, but which now housed a tractor. He felt a pang of regret. A horse would have been nice. Learning to ride a horse would have taken a lot of this endless time, and, if he learned, he could ride all over the land.

"Who is yonder knight on that great white horse?"

He would surely feel like Lancelot himself on the back of a horse. But the girl would be watching. She would already know how to ride, and so she would laugh when the horse balked or kicked, or worse yet, when he fell off into the manure. Someone should have warned him about her.

And whatever you do, speak not to the lady, nor turn aside at her request, for though she feigns a seemly countenance and pleads for your protection, she is in truth Morgana le Fay her very self, and has set for any knight who passes that way a cunning and deadly enchantment.

He didn't even know her stupid name, only that she was here before him, Parkington Waddell Broughton the Fifth, claiming the springhouse as her own. Did that mean he couldn't ever go there? Nonsense. Wasn't he the heir? She had no right to deny him anything. It was his ancestors who had hacked this estate out of the Virginia wilderness. The kid wasn't even American, for crying out loud.

What was she? Why would Frank have some foreign kid around? Did she live with him? His grandfather certainly wouldn't have put up with her if he hadn't had that stroke. Park was sure of that. Parkington the Third wouldn't have put up for five minutes with that sassy little foreign squirt.

He was outside the largest of the barns. There was noise coming from it—animal and human. He went to the side and peeped through a crack between boards. Frank was sitting on a low stool milking a cow. Every now and then she would stamp a foot and almost kick the pail. Frank would murmur something to quiet her, and she would swish her long tail across his face but otherwise hold still.

He could only see Frank's back—his blue work shirt with the sleeves rolled to his elbows, his overall straps stretched taut between wide shoulders, his dark red neck bent toward the cow's flank. My father didn't look like that, Park thought. He was tan, but not red-neck tan. He wasn't just a farmer. He was a pilot—a bomber pilot—totally in control of a gigantic plane, high above the world. He didn't go around watching for cow shit. Park glanced down at his ruined sneakers. For a minute he thought he might vomit.

I'm only here to find out about my father. I don't have to stay the whole stinking two weeks. The thought of having to stay the two full weeks nearly choked him. He'd die if he had to stay. Nobody could make him stay. The other half of his Greyhound ticket was safe in the pocket of his suitcase. Any day he took a notion, he could just walk into town and hop a bus for D.C. Nobody could stop him.

Not that anyone would want to. It was clear neither Frank nor Mrs. Davenport would. He was like a giant splinter under their skin. They would let him be until he worked himself out. The girl was different. Why hadn't Frank told him about her? It didn't seem natural. Frank hadn't really told him about anything except that he'd upset his grandfather before he'd even met him. Okay, so he messed up a lot, but not before he'd even walked in the door. Here he was already a nuisance and a problem before he ever got off the stupid bus. And that was the only thing Frank had bothered to tell him.

Frank got up, picked up the bucket and a leg of the stool, and gave the cow a gentle jab with his elbow. The cow shuddered and moved slowly away, her jaw going sideways, reminding Park of the bored waitress in the bus station working over her wad of chewing gum while he tried to tell her about the fifty cents the blinking drink machine had eaten.

The man had moved out of Park's sight, but Park could hear the sound of pouring milk, and then Frank came back into view and seated himself beside another cow, talking sweet talk as he gently maneuvered into position under her flank and began the rhythmic pull of the long, pinkish-brown teats.

Ah, sometimes he longed for the simple life of the herdsman. No care except the next meal, no honor to preserve, no foes to challenge, no quests to undertake. But God had ordained it otherwise for him—

"Gotcha!"
Park jumped around, almost knocking the stupid girl to the ground. She caught herself, nimbly dancing about from

one rubber-thong-sandaled foot to the other. "Sneak!" she taunted. "Peeping Pork!"

His neck grew hot. If she'd been a boy, he would have slugged her. What would the laws of chivalry have to say about a knight who slapped a lady into a cow pie? Just thinking about it made him feel better. "Call me Park," he said, sounding in his own head like the son of a bomber pilot.

"Oooo," she said, "temper like hot peppers." He tried to tell himself her tone was slightly more respectful despite the words.

"Thanh!" It was Frank's voice from inside the barn, quiet, but you could tell he meant business. "You're supposed to be in here, girl."

She glanced quickly at Park, and then, without a word, ran around to a side door of the barn and disappeared. Park could hear Frank, not exactly scolding, but speaking firmly. She wasn't talking back to Frank. She must be starting to work, but out of Park's line of vision.

Park walked around the barn and went through the door, which she had left ajar. It led into a small room lined with tubs. There were tall metal cans standing in one corner and some kind of machinery set up along the wall opposite the door, something to do with milk, obviously, because a tall metal canister at one end was partly filled with foamy milk, and beside it a smaller canister held several inches of yellow cream.

To his left, there were a door and a window that looked out from the small room into the main part of the barn, where there were eight cows, two of which were being milked by Frank and the girl.

Frank must have heard him, because he spoke to him

quietly from the other side of his cow. "It's a separator," he explained. "Takes the cream outta the milk."

"Oh," Park said, annoyed that Frank wouldn't think he could figure that out for himself.

"You not make him milk," the girl complained sharply. Her cow stamped and swished its tail, as if bothered by the pitch of Thanh's voice.

Frank's remained gentle. "Thought I'd let him be company the first day," he said. Frank had a nice voice, friendly and a little bit shy. Not Park's father's voice, though. It would have been more authoritative, but nice, too. The smile in the snapshot was almost mischievous.

The girl snorted with displeasure. "He not know how." The cow stamped a back foot and moved away from the sound. It took the girl a moment or two to quiet her cow and drag her stool and bucket to the position the beast had shifted to.

"Keep your voice down, Thanh," Frank said quietly. Then to Park, "Want a lesson?"

Park shook his head. Not with her thirty feet away. *Tuhn?* What kind of name was that? There were lots of Orientals in his school, mostly refugees. Vietnamese, he decided, or Cambodian. They all looked alike to him—the people who had killed his father.

Frank got up, nudged the cow gently away, and brought the bucket into the separator room.

"I guess you met Thanh already," he said.

"Sort of," Park mumbled.

Frank smiled, half apologetically. "She takes a little getting used to." He spoke so quietly that Thanh could not hear, even though Park could see her straining to listen as she tugged away at her cow.

63

"How old is she?" Park whispered the question. He hadn't really meant to ask, but it was vital information somehow.

Frank cocked his head, as if figuring. "Ten? That seems right. Ten. No. Eleven. She had a birthday in March."

Park grinned and said softly, "I'm nearly twelve."

"That a fact?" Frank was obviously one of those grown-ups who thought age wasn't important. Except perhaps in machinery, because he went on, "Now this separator"—pouring his milk into it and flipping a switch to send the motor quivering into life—"this thing is nearly forty years old, but it's still humming." Groaning would have been a more accurate description. Frank turned a spigot above each canister. "You want to keep an eye on that milk canister and turn off this spigot when it's nearly full?"

"Sure," Park answered. He was pleased Frank was giving him something to do. He watched the can filling up, mostly, it seemed, with foam, while the other got a steady golden trickle. At home they drank only skim milk, Randy's attempt to keep him trim, so he was fascinated by the cream. He began to feel fat just looking at it. What did Frank do with it? You couldn't drink stuff like that. Maybe that was what you made ice cream out of. Coffee cream or whipped cream, of course. Maybe butter. Of course, butter. It was more butter color than milk color. But how could you be sure it was clean? He'd already run into plenty of evidence that cows were a mess. There were flies buzzing about this barn, and every now and then a bird swooped through. Pasteurized. Remember fourth-grade science? Louis Pasteur and the little kids with cowpox—

"Stupid!" The girl shut off the spigot and jerked away the milk can, foam sudsing down its side and onto the dirt floor of the barn. She kept muttering something in a foreign language that sounded like cussing while she dragged an

64

empty can from the other side of the room. "Frank!" she said louder than she ought to have. "Dumb fool let milk run over."

Park started forward to help her, but she stopped him with a look, wrestled the empty can into position herself, and turned the spigot on again. Then she lifted her own milking pail and emptied it into the separator receptacle. "What the matter with you?" she muttered as she worked. She wasn't teasing now, just furious with his incompetence. "You no milk. All you do look. That all you do. And can't do that! Can't do no simple thing like that!" When she said *that,* her *th*'s were more like *z*'s, making her stage-whisper ranting sound like hornets.

He should have apologized. It was stupid of him not to keep his eyes on the can, but, well, if she hadn't treated him so—

He turned and left the barn. Let them watch their own stupid separator. They'd gotten along before he came. They didn't need him now. Or ever.

CASTLE UNDER CURSE

·7·

He went slowly up the hill toward the house, kicking a loose stone ahead of him, watching very carefully where he stepped.

"Stay!" the old man said. "I am sent to warn you. Do not take this path. Many the fair knights who went this way, never to return."

"But it is my quest. I must journey to yon castle and rescue the knights who lie chained in its dungeon."

"You go at peril of your life."

"That is as it may be. I go, nonetheless." He spurred

his mount and headed for the towers gleaming above the trees. The old man bowed in humble awe and watched until the noble forms of man and horse were long hidden by the forest green. His may be, thought the knight, the last friendly voice I hear in this world. But he did not allow himself fear or regret. He pressed onward to his danger.

"Back so soon?" Mrs. Davenport was on the back porch and saw him through the screen before he saw her. For an awful moment, he hoped he hadn't been moving his lips. He used to play his scenes aloud, but someone heard him one day, and he had to pretend that the person he was talking to was hiding behind a hedge. Since then he'd played them out in his head. "I think Mr. Frank's milking now," she continued. "The barn right at the bottom of the hill."

Park nodded. "I saw him." Jupe wandered over and sniffed his hand. Park hesitated, then reached under and scratched his neck. Jupe wagged his tail. "Good dog you got here," Park said.

"Jupe? I suppose. If you're the kind of person who likes dogs. I've always wanted a cat, myself. My daughter has three. They're so sweet. My little grandson carries them around and loves them like they're stuffed. Dresses them. Anything. They love him. Well," she laughed, "actually, everybody loves that child. Don't get me started on him. I thought about bringing one of the kittens here, but—" She jerked her head to the left.

"Frank says our little friend in there wouldn't allow one in the house. Just barn cats around here, and they're wild as tigers. Nothing like a nice house cat."

Park gave Jupe a final pat and went onto the back porch.

Mrs. Davenport was shelling fresh peas into a colander on her broad lap. She paused, sniffed the air, and then looked down her short nose at his sneakers. "Well," she said, "looks like our city boy has had his first big adventure."

Park blushed.

"We can hose those off in the yard," she said.

He found the hose attached to the back of the house. He turned it on and aimed it at his toes. The cold water splashed up. His jeans would be soaked. He threw down the hose and took off his sneakers, then his socks. Even after he'd washed the sneakers and wiped them on the grass, they were green, but the smell was not so strong. His feet looked enormous and sickly white like slabs of raw fish, but it couldn't be helped. He turned off the water, picked up his socks and wet sneakers, and tiptoed gingerly across the stubbly grass and gravelly path back onto the porch.

"Now we feel lots better, don't we?"

He made a yeslike sound and started to go around her toward his room when she asked, "You meet that girl yet?"

He nodded. There could only be one girl who rated that raised eyebrow and tone of voice.

"Little spitfire, isn't she?"

Park grinned slightly.

"Well, sonny, don't let her get you upset. She's like one of those barn kittens at first—all claws and teeth—but once you let her know who's boss—"

Did the housekeeper mean that he was supposed to lord it over Thanh? Somehow he didn't think so. She meant Frank, probably, or perhaps herself, though that seemed less likely.

"I guess you got to feel sorry for her a bit," she went on, nodding at a stool in a corner of the porch. Park dragged it over and sat beside her. She was, after all, a talker, and she just might be the one to tell him the answers to questions he didn't even know enough to ask.

"Yeah?" he said to urge her to keep on talking.

"Well, I suppose your Uncle Frank told you he and that woman are expecting." It was curious how everyone assumed someone else had told him something. What woman? Frank was married to the girl's mother? It was hard to believe. "She—the girl has been the only one for two years now. You got to figure she's scared to death Frank will forget her when he's got a kid of his own." It was true. Frank *was* married to the little geek's mother. He watched Mrs. Davenport's thumb go down the seam of a pod, popping the peas expertly into the colander. She had large red hands with blunt nails, but the motion was graceful. "Of course, she doesn't know Frank if she thinks that. Frank Broughton is as faithful as the day is long."

It was a nice expression. Whatever else Frank might be, he liked thinking of his father's brother as enduringly faithful.

"Uh—my father—was my father like Frank?" He hadn't meant to ask, not so soon anyway. The question just popped out like a pea from the pod.

"I never knew your daddy, sonny. He had already passed on before I came to work here."

"Oh." She couldn't know how disappointment blammed him in the chest.

"I came up here from Roanoke when"—again the jerk of the head toward the south room—"when he had his second stroke, about the time Frank got married." She leaned toward him. "That was a set-to in this county, let me tell you. A Broughton marrying one of them. Broughton has always been a big name around here. You got to admire the man. Loses

70

his tenants, his daddy has a stroke, the neighbors won't hardly speak, but he goes right ahead and gets married. I guess he thinks he knows what he's doing. They hardly been in America three, four months at the time. I mean to tell you, there was talk. Your uncle made like it didn't matter what people say. And here's Sada Davenport walking right into the middle not knowing anything about anything." She shook her head, as though remembering. "I wouldn't leave him. I don't mean I understand why a nice, polite, good-looking American gentleman would want to get himself—" Park leaned closer to her, but the sound of Frank talking to Jupe in the yard had shut her up. She straightened as Frank opened the screen door.

"Here you are," he said to Park, smiling his shy half smile. "I was afraid Thanh had chased you away for good." He went into what Park assumed must be the kitchen and returned minutes later with his pail empty. "I brought you whole milk tonight, Sada," he said.

"Not too much, I hope. That little Kelvinator isn't big enough for much of anything."

"About a half gallon." He started for the opposite door. "I'll just stop in and speak to the Colonel before I go."

She nodded. "Tell him not to fret. His supper will be there in a twinkle."

Frank gave Park a pained smile as he disappeared through the door. "How are you this evening, Colonel?" Then the Colonel's bedroom door was closed, and Park couldn't hear anything else.

After the peas were shelled, Park followed Mrs. Davenport into the hot, old-fashioned kitchen. There were potatoes boiling on an old stove, an old-time refrigerator with coils on top, and a single, stained sink under a window that looked over the front yard and toward the vegetable garden and Frank's house on the other side.

"Oh, my dear," the housekeeper said. "I should have sent these pods down when Frank was slopping the pigs. Well, they can wait." She set a small pan of water on for the peas and took a cooked chicken out of the refrigerator and began to saw off slices and arrange them on three plates.

"Can I help?" Park asked.

"Well, that's sweet of you. I could use help around here." She told him to set the table for two in the dining room. In the end he had to ask so many questions about where everything was that it would have been far easier for her to do it herself. Park concentrated on remembering what she told him, so that the next time he might be more help than bother. If he could trade help for information—

When the peas had turned from bright to grayish green, she mashed some of them with potatoes and minced chicken on one of the plates. "I'll be back as soon as I can." She sighed and rolled her eyes. "Let's hope we feel like cooperating with Sada tonight."

She was gone for more than a half hour, but, finally, supper was served. The chicken looked tough and cold, but hunger would help. Park cut the meat small and mixed it with the potato. Mrs. Davenport was watching, her mouth half open, like a mother holding a spoon poised in front of a stubborn baby.

Park stuck in a bite and smiled at her. "Good," he lied. He maneuvered the fork carefully around the great mound of overcooked peas, stockpiled on the right side of his plate like sickly green cannonballs.

She noticed. "We haven't taken a single bite of our nice vegetables," she said.

He strained to smile and slid his fork under three peas, reaching at the same time for the milk glass. There was no need to taste them, after all. He could always swallow—

He gagged. It was as though he'd tried to swallow a tablespoon of pure whipping cream. He managed to keep peas and milk from sputtering out of his mouth, but tears sprang to his eyes, and he choked as he forced everything down.

She leaned forward as though concerned, but he thought he read amusement in her eyes. "You city boys never tasted real milk, now have you?"

"It's all right," he squeaked. "Went down the wrong way."

"Dear, dear." She took a dainty bite of her own dinner.

He put the glass down and wiped his mouth on a yellow paper napkin. She was looking at him, so he put the napkin back in his lap and rooted in his pockets, his seat half off the chair, until he located a weary Kleenex, with which he wiped his eyes behind his glasses and then, as unobtrusively as he could, blew his nose.

She had stopped eating, just watched him, her fork in midair. Park gave a weak smile. "I guess I'm not very hungry. Too much junk on the bus or something."

"Well, we do need to be careful about that, don't we?" She took a bite and began chewing.

Released for the moment, he folded his napkin and put it beside his plate. Now what? He looked about the room so as not to seem to stare at her while she ate. The wallpaper was old and torn in one corner. Someone had patched it, but not too successfully. It was a large floral pattern—faded roses with ivy. He tried to imagine the woman who had chosen it. His grandmother? The Colonel's wife? No image came. Strange he never thought about her, only him.

"How is the—my grandfather?" The question squirted out. He hadn't planned, hadn't meant to ask.

"Oh, dear," she said. "I don't know." She stared for a moment at the potato on her fork. "I don't know. About the same, I guess." As though Park had any notion of what "same" was. Still, that had to mean that the old man was no longer upset about Park's arrival, didn't it? Wasn't "same" better than "upset"? Or did she mean he was still upset? Tomorrow, Park decided, I'll ask her to let me go in and see him. By tomorrow I'll get her liking me so she'll trust me and know I won't upset him. Although just thinking about going into that room sent a chill through him.

"Have you called your mother yet? Your Uncle Frank said earlier you ought to call her."

"Oh, yeah." He got up from the table. "I'd better do that now."

"The phone's right there in the kitchen beside the sink."

He called collect. Randy answered before the second ring. "Pork?" she said.

"Will you accept a collect call from Park Broughton?" the operator asked.

"I was worried—"

"Madame, will you accept a collect call—"

"Of course. When you didn't call at five—"

"Go ahead, please."

"Mom?"

"You're okay? Everything's all right?"

He glanced through the doorway at Mrs. Davenport, placidly chewing away. He had been so eager for an excuse to get up from the table he hadn't realized that she'd be sitting there, listening in.

"Sure, I'm fine," he said quietly.

"Your voice sounds funny."

"No, really. I'm fine. How're things with you?"

"Oh, I'm all right. Relieved. Why didn't you call at five? I came home from work early so I'd be here."

"I'm sorry. I guess we were milking," he whispered, his hand cupped around the mouthpiece.

"Milking?" She was laughing in disbelief. "Frank's got you working already?"

"Yeah," he lied.

"How is Frank?"

"He's fine. Mom—" He looked at Mrs. Davenport. Her eyes were cut sideways toward the kitchen. Park moved as far away from the door as the cord would allow. "Mom, you didn't tell me my dad had a brother."

"Who? Frank? I'm sure I did. You just forgot."

She had not told him. He would have remembered something like that. "You didn't tell me about anything." She was quiet for so long that he thought they'd been cut off. "Mom? Are you there?"

"I'm here. How's the Colonel?" she asked finally.

"About the same." Well, that was all they would tell him except that he was upset, and he wasn't going to tell his mother that.

"I see," she said, as though the words made any sense. Another long pause. "Pork?"

"Yeah?"

"I am going to talk to you about your father—soon as you're old enough."

Mom, he wanted to yell, I'm almost twelve, but he couldn't, not with Mrs. Davenport right there, stretching her neck out like an accordion to catch his whispered words.

"I love you, son. Don't forget that."

"Sure," he said dully. "It's okay. Well, I'll call you in a couple of days."

"Whenever you need to. You going to be all right there, bud?"

"I'm fine," he whispered fiercely. "Don't worry." Then in a loud, cheerful voice for Mrs. Davenport's benefit, "Okay, then. I'll be in touch. Bye."

AT THE SPRINGHOUSE

·8·

He woke with the first light. For a minute he lay still in the tall bed and tried to remember where he was. A rooster's proud, high call was answered by a low moo. Then he retrieved his glasses from the nightstand, threw back the sheet and cotton blanket, and slid onto the floor. His mother had bought him pajamas so he wouldn't have to sleep in his underwear at the relatives', but the material was a thin cotton polyester mix that lay cold against his skin. It was a long way to the bathroom without a robe. He dressed quickly, except for his stained sneakers, and, with his toothbrush and paste in hand, began to creep sock footed across the hall toward the staircase.

He kept his ears strained for the sound of someone awake (on farms, didn't people get up with the dawn?) and then realized that no one in this huge house would be expected to rise early—an invalid, a puff-brained housekeeper, and a useless city kid. At the bottom of the stairs just beyond the grandfather clock was the closed, heavy wooden door. Behind it lay Parkington Waddell Broughton the Third, or what was left of him.

A miracle! The lad simply entered, laid his hand upon the King's forehead, and the old one sat up and called for his sword. Healed! Healed! Simply the touch of that young hand, the bonds of love and kinship proving far stronger than the bonds of illness or death. Simply the touch of that pure young—

Park forced himself to turn right and go toward the bathroom. He took extra care with his teeth, so as to make it take twice as long as usual. Now. What was he going to do with the rest of the hours? He looked at his watch. Five seventeen. Five seventeen? There was no use going back to bed. He was wide awake. Amongst the clutter of the back porch he found a pair of rubber boots that were only a little too large for his feet and let himself carefully out the screen door, closing it gently so it wouldn't slam.

He breathed in the bright, crisp air. He'd never been outside so close to a summer dawn before. Outdoors he could hear even more clearly the early-morning cackle and murmur of the animals. Jupe came loping across from the doghouse to sniff Park's hand. He lowered his head for Park to scratch.

"Good boy," he whispered. "Good old Jupe." Jupe wagged his tail. Park took a deep breath. There was no evil in the air this morning. He stood straight.

I shall go down among the cottages and make my rounds before I break my fast. The seneschal is in every way a worthy steward, but when I return from questing, the peasants' hearts are gladdened by the sight of their lord. He nodded, touching his noble forehead to the young maid gathering eggs and to the young lad carrying food to the pigsty. He would just stop and greet the plowmen heading for the fields and then go down to his springhouse for a drink of its wonderful cool water. "When in castle," the peasants would say, "the master does not begin a day without a drink from the spring."

As he passed the sty, the pigs waddled toward the trough, bumping one another's mud-coated bodies, squealing expectantly. He gave them a bow. "Alas, poor pigs," he said, cocking his head toward Jupe and laughing a gentle, pitying laugh. Jupe gave him a puzzled stare.

Thanh was not there to watch him climb the fence, but he had the dog, so he carefully cracked open the gate and held it to let Jupe pass through and then competently slipped through himself and rehung the wire loop over the gatepost.

Why did the farm smell so much better this morning? The cow piles were still there, but he could only smell them if he concentrated. The air was clean and sweet, almost as clean and sweet as the water from the spring. The sun was climbing higher, scrubbing the sky to a radiant blue. Something jiggled in his chest, making him want to jump and run. That's what he'd do to pass the endless days. He'd run. He'd grow two inches and lose twenty pounds. No, then he might not be big enough for junior high football. Not lose weight, just turn any suggestion of flab into muscle, that's what he'd do. Starting now. This moment. He went off the dirt road into the patchy grass and found a place clean of rocks and manure. One hundred push-ups every morning before breakfast! That's what he'd do! The grass was wet, but he wasn't going to let that stop him.

One. Two. Three. He pushed quickly from his hands. Four. Fiiiive. At six he could barely lift his hips out of the grass, and at seven he sprawled facedown in the dampness, his chest heaving. Perhaps he needed to work up slowly to a hundred. He should have been working out all year instead of reading so much. How many times had Greg said that? And Greg was right. What good did it do a guy to be big for his age if he was too much of a slob to make the football team?

The cold wet was seeping through his T-shirt, and Jupe was nosing his neck. Park got up, but not without a quick look around to make sure no one had seen him. He gave Jupe a scratch behind the ears and went on across the grass to the springhouse.

His hand was on the door when he heard the sound. Someone was inside—hardly five thirty in the stinking morning and someone was inside crying their heart out. It had to be Thanh. Hard as it was to imagine that tough little stick bawling, Park was sure it was she. Jupe gave a low whine. Park put out his hand to still the dog, but it was too late. The girl jerked open the door so abruptly that he and Jupe nearly fell over the threshold.

"You!" she cried out. "What you do here? My place! You no peek! No peek!" She threw out her arm as if to hit him, but he jerked away, and she fell to her knees, crying in rage and frustration.

He felt sorry, but not altogether sorry. She had certainly shown him no sympathy. "Hey," he said in the gentlest voice he could manage. "It's okay. I'm not going to tell anybody I saw you."

But she didn't stop crying or banging the ground with her fists. "Why you come? Why you come?"

To the farm? To the springhouse? What did she mean? "To get a drink of water," he said. It seemed the simplest answer.

"Lie! Lie!"

"I woke up early." His voice was testy. "I wanted a drink of water." He stepped around her into the springhouse and pushed the door closed behind him. The little geek. Who was she calling a liar?

He sat down on the edge of the trough to collect himself. He wasn't going to turn over the springhouse to her. It was not hers.

And if I must, I will challenge that black knight upon a field of honor, from which one of us will never rise again except he be borne away upon a death litter. For I will ask no quarter, nor shall I grant any to so foul a foe—

As if in reply, she threw open the door, which banged against the inside wall, making the whole little frame structure shudder.

"What you do?" she demanded.

"I'm getting a drink of water, like I said."

"Where your cup?"

"I—"

She jerked her head. "Stupid. Use coconut."

"I know that."

"I show," she said, snatching the shell off the ledge above the pipe. "Move self."

81

"I know how to get a drink."

"I say, move fat self. I show."

He moved all right. He moved right out of the spring-house and started up the road. Jupe stood still, his head going from the open door of the springhouse to the boy, like an onlooker at a tennis match.

Park whistled. "Come on, boy," he said. The dog hesitated a moment, then turned and loped up the road toward him. Park straightened his shoulders. Was she watching? Of course she would be. He turned his back on the springhouse and went to the farmhouse without a backward glance. That should show her.

Just as he got through the swinging picket fence, he changed his mind. "Stay, Jupe," he said and raced down to the main barn, where, sure enough, Frank was milking away all by himself.

"Can I help?" Park was careful to make his voice sincere, but gentle, so as not to disturb the temperamental cows.

Frank greeted him with a grin. "Sure. Go wash your hands and get yourself a stool. I'll show you."

Somehow it was all right when Frank said it. "See, here? You give it a little squeeze at the top and then just sorta strip the milk down the pipe. You try."

The cow's freckled teat was warm and surprisingly rough under his hand. He squeezed and pulled. Nothing happened.

"Don't worry," Frank said. "You'll get the hang of it. Keep trying."

He squeezed and pulled and squeezed and stripped and squeezed and yanked and finally, finally, spied a tiny trickle of white stuff. "I did it! I did it!" The cow stamped and whipped him in the face with her tail.

"Whoa, easy," said Frank. "Now this next time, head the milk into the bucket and you'll be on your way."

In the crevice of Frank's big work boot, just past the laces, lay a little puddle of milk. Park stared at it. He couldn't speak. His face was burning up. Frank shook his foot. "Okay, try once more." Without looking up or around, Park tugged once more at the teat. Nothing again. He was getting hotter. He grabbed the teat with his right hand and stripped with his left. Milk came out all right, but the cow stamped and switched. "Gentle," said Frank. "A little more patience."

Behind him Park could hear the door open and close. Thanh was at the edge of his vision, patting a cow's rump into position, dragging a stool and bucket into place. She started a rhythmic, two-handed *ping pang, ping pang* into her metal pail.

"Easy, now. Gentle. Firm, though," Frank was saying in his ear, the *ping pang, ping pang* like a saucy piccolo obbligato to Frank's bass voice. Park concentrated all his attention on the freckled teat and the weak stream of warm milk he was intermittently coaxing from it into Frank's already half-filled pail. He wasn't going to let that little geek—that was the word, wasn't it?—*geek*. It was a word that stretched his mouth into a smile just to think it. Geek. Geek. Geek. He pinched the teat. Geeeek. He pulled down the length of it. Geek geeeek, geek geeeek, geek geeeek.

"One hand," Thanh was muttering. "Can only one hand."

Frank ignored her. "That's the ticket," he said to Park. He stood up, picking up his stool. "Okay. You finish this one, and I'll start another."

Park nodded happily. Geek geeeek. Geek geeeek. The *ping pang* to his left had turned into *pssss pssss*. Thanh's milk was now hitting milk instead of metal. No matter. Geek geeeek. It was as satisfying to say the words inside his head as it would have been to give her the finger. Geek geeeek. He tried stripping the teat with his left hand. Nothing. With his right hand, he could manage a tiny stream. But it looked better to sit there with both hands on separate teats, so he went ahead pulling left and right in rhythm, even though nothing at all was hitting the pail from the teat in his left hand, and from the right there was barely more than a thread of milk.

Frank finished his second cow and got up to empty the bucket. Thanh got up as well. Show-off. Frank glanced into her bucket. "Sure you emptied that bag?" he asked quietly.

"Sure," she snapped. "I finish."

"It's not a race, Thanh."

"I say, finish."

"Give it a few more pulls, okay? It's hard on the old cow to leave—"

"Okay. Okay. I do."

Geek geeeek. Geek geeeek. Got you. Frank did know how to keep the little barn cat in her place. Park loved it. He leaned his forehead against the cow's brown and white flank to hide his smirk. That's what she got for trying to show off. Geek geeeek. Geek geeeek.

"How we doing?"

"Uh. Okay, I guess." Park looked down quickly to make sure there was no milk on the dirt floor of the barn.

"You got a good rhythm going. Little more strength in those hands, and I'll have me a real milker."

Park blushed. Out of the corner of his eye he could see Thanh getting up from her stool and stomping into the separator room with her pail. He didn't care. It wasn't a race, Frank had said. Besides, with a little practice he'd be faster than she was anyhow. His hands were twice as big as hers, and he had something she didn't. Desire.

TAKING UP ARMS

·9·

Mrs. Davenport poured milk from a big jug in the refrigerator, then swirled a teaspoon around the glass before setting it down on the kitchen table in front of Park. The cream still clogged the raw milk. He gagged. He couldn't help it.

"You city boys seem to like it homogenized," she said, watching him with an amused expression.

He shook his head. His mother had shifted to skim the minute she saw an extra pound on his body, but he wasn't going to tell Mrs. Davenport that. Farm people liked fat kids, didn't they? "It's fine," he muttered.

She handed him a big plate with two fried eggs still

swimming in the cooking grease and thick bacon barely streaked with lean. "Biscuits're coming," she said.

He would have to drink the milk to wash down the eggs, but he didn't know if he could manage without gagging again. She was standing there, hand on hip, pursed smile on her pink and powdered face, as though she was going to watch him eat every last bite. Finally she turned back to the stove and began to arrange a plate for the sickroom. The old man got a chopped-up soft-boiled egg and a cup of coffee and, when she pulled the biscuits from the huge stove, a margarined biscuit with a little jam, which she cut into bite-sized pieces.

"Be back," she said. "Let's hope we feel like eating our breakfast this morning."

He half rose from the table. "Can I help? Take his food in, or—"

"Oh, no, not today," she said. "Therapist comes on Thursdays. He's always extra nervous when the therapist's coming." Her tone of voice made it clear just how little she thought of the therapist.

He looked around for a place to dispose of his eggs. At least he could pour the milk down the sink. He did so quickly, and frantically splashed water around to clean the trace. The pig bucket! It was on the porch waiting for Frank to take it down to the sty. He chopped and sloshed the eggs and bacon until no one could have recognized them, picked up a handful of peapods, poured in his breakfast, rearranged the peapods on top, replaced the lid on the bucket. Whew. She wasn't back, so he helped himself to a couple of hot biscuits. These he slathered with butter and jam and ate standing up. A nice glass of skim or even homogenized milk would have made them taste less dry, but even so, they made a decent breakfast.

Mrs. Davenport still had not returned when he finished, so he rinsed his plate and glass and silverware and stacked them neatly beside the sink. Looking out of the window, he could see the house across the garden. As he watched, the front door opened and a woman stepped out onto the small porch. She was too far away for Park to see her face, but she was, as they say in the Christmas story, great with child. Thanh's mother. Frank's wife. Though Park still had trouble believing that Frank would marry one of them.

She had a throw rug in her hands, and she was shaking it over the railing. She stopped and turned toward the open door, as though talking to someone. Then Frank came out. After a few more words, he took the rug from her. She seemed to be protesting, but Frank put a hand on her shoulder and guided her back inside. He closed the door behind them. Just like an ordinary husband worried about his pregnant wife.

A few seconds later Frank came around the back of the house. He had a straw hat on his head. He crossed the field that lay beyond the vegetable garden and the front-yard fence and disappeared down the hill in the direction of the barns. He had no sooner gone than the woman came out again and began shaking the rug for all she was worth. Well, you could tell she was kin to Thanh, now couldn't you? Poor Frank, with two of them to manage.

Park watched until she had finished her chore and re-entered the little house. What now? He wandered out onto the back porch, wondering what to do with all the rest of the day. Here he was on a farm that should have been his kingdom, and he felt more like a prisoner than anything else. Why had they said he could come at all if they had no intention of allowing him to enjoy himself? He wouldn't have minded not being entertained if he had been free to explore, but that little—little geek kept popping up. Geek geeeek. He had to smile, remembering the milking.

He spied the gun rack then, in the far right corner, almost hidden behind a clothes tree hung with old raincoats and winter jackets. Park went over to it and moved the clothes tree to one side. He'd always wanted a gun. Ever since he could remember, he'd begged for one. His mother always said that you couldn't have a gun in the city, but that wasn't really it. She wouldn't even allow him a pop gun. She was hysterical on the subject of guns. Three years ago she'd found the toy one he had traded his baseball cards for, and she'd screeched as though he'd wounded her. She left the house at nine o'clock at night, just to make sure she disposed of it where he could never ever find it. And here they were— eight rifles lined up in a glass cabinet. He went over and tugged at the knob. Locked. Just his luck.

He knew what he'd do. He'd ask Frank. That would prove how mature and responsible he was. He'd ask Frank to teach him how to handle and shoot a gun. Men loved to do things like that. Real men. Frank would get a bang (hah!) out of teaching him.

He found Frank in the shed, pouring gas into the tank of the tractor. "Anything I can do?" Park asked politely. He wanted Frank to realize how eager he was to help.

"Oh, I don't—"

"I know I don't know much"—he tried to sound humble—"about farming. But I want to learn. Really, I do."

Frank put down the gas can, capped it, and then screwed a cap back onto the tractor tank. "Did you have something particular in mind?"

"Oh, I don't know. I just hate to feel I'm only in the

88

way." That was the wrong thing to say. If Frank didn't already think that, he would now, for sure.

"Well, okay. Thanh's weeding the vegetable garden. You could give her a hand if you like."

Not what he'd had in mind at all. "Sure," he said. "And sometime . . ."

"Yeah?"

"Well, I've always wanted to learn how to—well, I've never had the opportunity, living in the city—but I mean, if I'm going to be here for two weeks—"

Frank's eyebrow was going higher with every phrase. Park rushed to the point. "Would you teach me how to shoot?"

Frank hesitated, but only for a second. "All right," he said. "I guess it can't hurt you to learn some respect for a gun."

Park reddened with pleasure. "I swear," he said, "I'll be really careful. I'll do just what you say."

"I'll be up to the house about three thirty. Before milking."

"Thank you."

"I'd just as soon you not make a big thing of this with Thanh."

"Oh, no, sir. Of course not. Girls don't like guns."

"Girls who've been shot at don't tend to, no."

She was sitting on her haunches pulling weeds out from around the pea vines when he found her, the red baseball cap pushed back on her head and underneath, her hair plastered to her small brown face with sweat.

"Frank told me to help."

She looked up at him when he spoke, her eyes sparkling. "You help me?"

"Yeah."

89

"I *show* you," she said.

"Okay." He was not going to let her ruffle him.

She stood up. "You do here." She indicated the spot where she had been squatting. "You pull everything don't walk up pole."

He nodded and started to work without a word. The thought of that row of guns in the glass cabinet could keep him going for quite a while. It was as though they had been waiting there just for him.

Park was on the porch well before three thirty. He heard a car drive up to the front gate and Jupe's warning bark, then at the doorway Mrs. Davenport's greeting and a sharp, businesslike woman's voice reply . . . their voices as they came down the hall . . . the woman's greeting at his grandfather's door . . . the closing of the door.

Just then Frank came swinging around the corner of the house. Park opened the screen door for him. "You remembered."

"I keep my word, as a rule," he said quietly.

"Oh, I didn't mean—"

Frank went past him into the kitchen. Park heard him open a drawer, and then he returned to the porch with a key ring in his hand. He fiddled keys through his thumb and forefinger until he found the one he was looking for. He unlocked the cabinet, took out the smallest of the rifles, and handed it to Park.

"This one here is a single-shot, open-sight twenty-two," he said. "Youth size."

He must have sensed Park's reaction because he went on. "It's a good starting gun, but that doesn't mean it's a toy. You can kill a person with it if you don't know how to respect it."

"Yessir," Park mumbled, feeling he needed to assure Frank of his respect.

With a second key Frank unlocked the lower wooden doors and took out a small cardboard box of ammunition. Then he relocked both doors, pocketed the keys and ammunition, and took back the gun. "Target's already in the jeep," he said. "I figure we'd better ride over to the far pasture. We won't bother anybody over there."

After the first gate, Frank sat at the wheel and let Park jump out to open and reclose each gate. It was a long, bumpy ride, and by the time Frank had shut off the motor and pulled on the hand brake, they were several hills away from the farmhouse, near a large shedlike barn, which was worn gray with age. Sheep approached them and began to nuzzle the jeep. "We're disappointing them," Frank said. "They think we brought salt."

It seemed to take forever. First there was a repeat of the speech on "a gun is not a toy." Then Frank took the gun apart and showed Park how to clean it and reassemble it. Then he taught him the name of every bump on the barrel. Next he showed him how to load and unload. He made Park rehearse the procedures several times.

Okay. Okay. I've got it. Now let's shoot. But he didn't dare say it aloud. At long last he was permitted to put the gun on his shoulder with the safety still in place.

"First you find your target. Then you aim at it, making sure you can see the front sight right there in the middle groove of the rear sight, okay?"

They didn't line up, no matter what he did.

Frank laughed. "Try squinting your left eye and sighting with your right."

Park blushed and switched eyes. It worked.

"Wait, now." Did Frank sense how impatient he was?

91

His uncle went to the jeep and out of the back pulled a bale of hay, which he set on a low stump. On the end of the bale was attached a faded target of circles within circles. There was a number on each circle. He could read five on the outside and twenty-five in the center. The other numbers were peppered with holes. "Your dad and I about wore this out, but it'll do for now, I expect."

Your dad and I. The very same target his father had learned to shoot at. Park began to shake. The very same gun, probably. The very same gun.

"With a low target like this," Frank was saying, "you'll do better lying on your stomach. Now what's the most important thing you're going to remember about a gun?"

"Not to shoot myself?"

"Good boy. Nor me either." He grinned. "Now check to make sure the safety's pushed forward until you're actually ready to shoot. Okay, wait a minute." Frank walked toward the sheep, who were standing like spectators at the eighteenth hole of a golf tournament. "Shoooo. Shoo. Git!" He waved his arms, and they trotted obediently over the hill and out of sight. Frank smiled at Park and continued directions as he came back toward him. "Safety still on? Good. Okay, now. Line up the sights with the center of the target. No rush. Just take your time. Take your time." He was behind Park's left shoulder. "You can release the safety and fire whenever you're ready," he said quietly.

The box was dangerously low of ammunition before Park was able even to hit the target, but Frank seemed not to mind. "Okay," he'd say, "that was better. Okay, close."

At last—"Hey, hold your fire. I think we got a five there." He went over to the target and stuck his finger on it. "Yep. Brand-new hole. Nice going."

In his pleasure, Park missed the next several times, but

after another five, Frank began closing the ammo box. "Milking time," he said. "We can't keep the ladies waiting. Now. You and I both know that this gun only holds one cartridge at a time and you've already shot it, but it's a good habit to always treat a gun like it's loaded. All right. Open the bolt and make sure the chamber's empty. That's right. Now you put the bolt back in place and push the safety forward. That's the ticket. Okay, why don't you put the gun in the back of the jeep while I carry this target up to the barn for next time?"

"This was great," Park said. "Can next time be tomorrow?"

"We'll see," Frank answered, but his head was nodding yes as he said it.

Park woke in the night, too excited to sleep well. He lay in the big bed, taking imaginary aim at his father's old target. This time his first three shots hit fives, then tens. At last— bull's-eye! *"That's my boy!"* He turned at the sound of the proud shout to see a suntanned man in an aviator's cap, grinning at him with pleasure.

He wondered if Frank had put the keys to the gun cabinet back in the kitchen drawer. His uncle had gone into the kitchen after he'd locked up the gun, but Park hadn't followed. He didn't want Frank to think he was snooping around to see where he kept the keys. Park certainly wouldn't use the gun without Frank being there, but still, he couldn't help wondering. It would prove that Frank trusted him, wouldn't it, if he left the keys right there in the same place?

Suddenly he couldn't stay in bed any longer. He was as restless as his old hamster, which had run his mother crazy racing its tiny wheel *plickety plickety plickety* all night long. She'd made Park give it away. Then she felt bad and bought him a goldfish. Ever try to snuggle a goldfish? It died—not from snuggling—neglect, more likely.

Park threw off the covers and grabbed a sweat shirt against the night chill. In the city it never got cold on a summer night. Some nights he'd lie in his sweat, hardly able to breathe. He tiptoed down the stairs.

As he reached the bottom step, he heard something that went right through him, nailing him to the floor. He'd never heard a grown-up cry out loud in real life, maybe on TV, but not like this.

Park crept to the bedroom door and put his ear against the wood. Yes. The old man was in there sobbing, sobbing his heart out. What could it be? Was he in pain? Was he lonely? Was he angry? What could be so terrible that a man who had spent his life in the army—a colonel, a veteran (as Park was sure) of many battles—what could reduce a soldier and a hero to sobbing aloud in the middle of the night?

For the second time in one day, he was standing outside a door and listening to another person weep. *Peek, Pork.* He shouldn't, he knew. It was none of his business. But for goodness' sake, this wasn't some foreign brat in there; it was his grandfather, his namesake. Shouldn't he do something? Shouldn't he call Mrs. Davenport or Frank? Shouldn't he— shouldn't he crack open that heavy door and just make sure everything was all right?

His hand squeezed the knob. Did he imagine it? Or were the sobs really louder and more wrenching? He drew back. How would I like it if some stranger busted in on me while I was crying? And I'm just a kid. But suppose he needs help? Suppose he has some awful pain and can't reach for a bell or whatever? Park hardly touched the knob. The door fell away from his hand.

There was a lamp on beside the bed, casting its light on a pillow. An empty pillow. Park's heart jumped for the ceiling. Then he saw him. The old man was on his feet, his swaying body humped over the metal frame of a walker. The sobbing cut off abruptly as the head twisted up sideways to look at the intruder.

Park opened his mouth, but it was stone dry. He meant to say something. Are you all right? What's the matter? Can I help? Anything.

Haaaa. The wail, for it was a wail, almost inhuman, the cry of some wretched animal in pain. *Haaaa.* Park turned and fled from the sound of it.

· 10 ·

He was cold. So cold he might never be warm again. He wanted to get up and get another blanket from the wardrobe, but he couldn't make himself move. If he took his head out from under the covers, he might hear that sound again.

He froze. *Haaaa. Haaaa.* So soft that he wasn't sure if he was imagining it. He shoved his head under a pillow and then covered the pillow with his blanket. *Haaaa. Haaaa.* He knew he was not to look. Do not open the door. Do not look in. But he had looked. He had seen the sight that no one could look upon and live.

The cold stabbed at his heart again. He curled his body against it, but nothing helped. He had looked, and now the curse was on him. Why, why had he opened that door? Why had he waked in the night? Why had he gone downstairs? Why, oh, God, why had he ever come to this terrible place?

His mother had not wanted him to come. She had tried to protect him, but he had demanded to know. Some things it is better not to know, but he had been too stupid and too stubborn to realize that. Standing in the February sun with his fingers on the shining black stone, he had thought it would all be wonderful—that the secret was a treasure, like the Grail, that his mother was jealous of. For if he once glimpsed it, he would be rich and noble, breaking free, soaring beyond her tight, miserly little life. But she had loved him after all. She had not wanted to keep him captive, but to protect him.

He did not remember there in his cold fear that she could not know how far the blight had crept, how near to walking death. Even if he had, it would not have mattered. She was the wise one. She knew the past should stay sealed. Hadn't she tried to stop him? He must thank her for that.

He wanted to go back to sleep, but his mind went on and on. Not as it usually did, painting scenes of adventure and conquest, but on and on into a wordy tangle of fears that had no clear faces—only a bent and shadowy ghost—*haaaa*.

Maybe he should play sick in the morning. He really felt sick. He had to get himself together. What if someone had seen him?

Someone *had* seen him. He would never be able to enter that room again. He would never see Parkington Waddell Broughton the Third. His grandfather had gone, leaving that thing in his place. The geeks had killed his father, and something or someone even more terrible had destroyed his grandfather. And somehow (though how?), somehow, it was his fault. As soon as the thought occurred to him, he recognized its truth. He had destroyed them both. Or rather God had, but it was because of Park that God had done it.

He tore into his mind for a logical explanation. After all, he'd been little more than a baby when his father died. It didn't make sense, and yet . . . For evidence, there was the way his mother behaved. She wanted to love him, she did love him, Park knew that, but there was that coldness inside her. It was because she couldn't forgive him for what he had done to his father. And what had happened to his grandfather—that happened because of what Park had made happen to his father. Grief had destroyed the old man, grief for his firstborn son. And it was all somehow Park's fault.

How could it be his fault? How? How? It was *her* fault. She was one of them—his father had been killed in her country, after all. It was her fault, not his. Or Frank's fault. Frank had stayed home safe and comfortable and let his brother go off to war. Then he'd married one of his brother's killers. Why couldn't it be Frank's fault? Or Randy's? Why hadn't she made his father stay home? Nobody had to serve two tours in 'Nam. Why had she let him go back again? If his father had been there the year Park was born, there was no way that he could have gotten killed there in 1973 unless she had let him go back. Maybe it was his father's fault. Maybe he wanted to go back. No. That was impossible. The fault was Park's own.

But I didn't mean to. I didn't. I didn't. He forced himself to be quiet in case God should be saying, at that very minute, "It's okay. Everything will be all right." God should know he hadn't meant to do whatever it was he must have done. Okay, God. Give me a sign that it's all right. That you don't blame me. Like if Mrs. Davenport was to walk in here right now to find out if I was okay.

Nobody came. But it was the middle of the night, for

crying out loud. Bad sign. Ask for something else. The
telephone will ring in the morning and it will be my mother
asking about me. No. Anytime tomorrow. No. Not my mother.
Somebody—anybody tells me it's okay, I'll know everything
will be all right.

He must have slept, for he sat up with a start. What time
was it? The sun was high, and Thanh stood grinning beside
his bed.

"You sleep in that?" She jabbed her finger into his chest.
He yanked at the sheet to make sure it covered his thin
pajama pants and then looked down at his sweat shirt. It was
his Friends of the National Zoo shirt with a large monkey
and the initials FONZ. Thank God he wasn't naked.

"What are you doing in here?"

She shrugged.

"Can't a guy have any privacy around here?"

She shrugged again. "I come wake you. You late."

The cold hit Park's stomach. "Where's Mrs. Davenport?"

"I dunno," she said. "Maybe with the grandfather." ("Zugh
granfahzuh" was the way she said it.)

So—everything was all right. Wasn't it? Nothing out of
the ordinary. He dared to ask. "He's all right?"

"I dunno. No tell me. Maybe not so good. She call Frank
come."

His stomach flopped over. No one could know about last
night, could they?

"When you get up?"

"When you get out," he said sharply. Oh, God, what had
he done?

She pinched her mouth in her sassy way, flung one little
hip around, and pranced out the door. He waited until she
was in the hall, jumped out of bed, and slammed the door.

Too late he knew he shouldn't have slammed it, but maybe it didn't sound so loud downstairs. Maybe with the heavy bedroom door shut, they would hardly hear it at all. He pulled on his jeans. His hands shook on the zipper, and he could barely manage the snap.

He crept down the stairs. At the foot he strained to hear through the closed door. There was a voice, Frank's voice, but the words were muffled through the thick wood. He rounded the banister. Thanh was sitting geek style on her haunches under the stairs. She grinned. "Why you spy?" she asked, obviously pleased to have caught him trying to eavesdrop.

"I wasn't spying," he said in a hoarse whisper.

She raised an eyebrow and then grinned again. "Okay to me," she said.

He walked past her into the dining room and through it into the kitchen. His place was still laid at the table, but there was no food. He opened the refrigerator door and stared in, but he couldn't think what to get out. He couldn't think at all.

"You head too hot?"

He jerked around. "No, my head is not too hot. I'm getting something to eat." He saw an apple, took it out, and shut the door. "You're in my way."

"Oh, excuse, Mister Cool Head"—she stepped aside—"but Frank say you come garden now."

"Aw right!" He took a vicious bite out of the apple. "I'm coming."

He finished weeding the peas, and after Thanh had overexplained what onion tops looked like, he squatted down to work on them. He wished he'd worn his damp sneakers after all. The rubber boots cooked his feet and chafed the backs of his legs against his jeans. The sun was beating down on his head, but he didn't stop, even to wipe the stupid perspiration that was running into his eyes.

"You need hat." She shoved her own red baseball cap back and wiped her face as she walked toward him.

Did that count as a sign from God? Probably not. Besides, she was some kind of heathen—all those people were. "I'm okay," he said, but he knew it didn't count if he had to say it himself.

"You want water?" She took a small thermos off a belt slung round her hips and held it out to him.

"Okay," he said, collapsing from his painful squatting position (how could geeks do it on and on?). Park waited for her to produce a cup, but there was none. He unscrewed the top of the jug. Oh, well, if he caught some Oriental disease, what did it matter? He was already cursed.

"He's dying, Mrs. Broughton. I'm afraid there is nothing I can do."

"Oh, doctor, no. Please let me speak to him. I have to tell him."

"He may not be able to hear you."

"But he must. He has to know that it's all right. That nothing is his fault. That no one blames him."

"If only you had told him sooner, Mrs. Broughton. I'm afraid now—"

"Don't be pig. I want water, too."

He held the thermos up to her, wiping his mouth on the back of his hand.

She took a cotton handkerchief from the pocket of her jeans and carefully polished the rim of the thermos before taking a long draft. "Old grandfather crazy today," she said.

He jerked to attention. "Who said?"

"Oh, Frank. He say my mother." She took another maddeningly long drink.

Park put his hand on the ground to steady himself. "Yeah?" He tried to make it casual. "Nobody said anything to me."

"They not say *you*!" She looked down at him with such contempt that he struggled to his feet so he could be the tall one again.

"What do you mean?" How could anyone know about last night?

"You just kid. They not say kid's old grandfather crazy. I hear."

He broke into a sweat of relief. She only meant they wouldn't *tell* him, not that anyone was thinking of blaming him.

"What do you mean 'crazy'?"

"Oh, you know, cry, cry, cry all time. He no talk so he cry everything." She giggled. "Like baby."

"It's not funny."

She shrugged.

"Anyhow, how do you know? I bet you never saw him."

"I see. When I come. Frank take me. 'This Thanh,' he say, and old grandfather cry so Frank take me 'way. But"— she cut her eyes at Park, and they were full of mischief— "but I tell you, I peek. They put him in push chair on porch sometime. I behind bush. Sometime even I look in window, but old grandfather see and cry, so I run like rabbit." She giggled.

"You shouldn't do that."

"Frank catch me. He mad maybe."

"No, I don't mean you shouldn't run, stupid. I mean you shouldn't spy in the first place."

"I like," she said stiffly.

"It's mean."

"Not mean. I want see."

"Well, you shouldn't."

She cocked her head. "You want see?"

He was sweating for real now.

"Your grandfather. You see."

"No."

"Next time. I come get you. We peek. You and me. Okay?"

"No!"

"No be 'fraid. He don't hurt."

"I'm not afraid."

"So? Okay. You show. We go now. Look in window."

"No. You said yourself he was all upset today."

"He not see. We see him. Come."

What could he do? He followed her toward the house, his feet heavy as tombstones, his heart shaking his whole rib cage. She led him around the picket fence. Jupe came racing across the yard, wagging his tail. "Shhhh!" she warned him. She pushed open the gate and signaled Park to follow. At the south corner of the house, the huge front porch made a little forward jog, right at the window of the downstairs bedroom. The corner had been planted with snowball bushes that were as tall as Park and bursting with blue and white blooms. Thanh grabbed his arm to lead him behind the bushes into the almost hidden bit of porch behind them. They crouched below the window, letting their breathing and heartbeats quiet.

Finally she raised her eyes to the sill. "Sleep," she said, sounding disappointed. If the old man was asleep, there was nothing to be afraid of, was there? Park inched up.

Park could see the bed. The sun from the window glinted on a metal triangle hung like a trapeze above it. And under the triangle the old man lay on his back against a high pillow, his eyes closed over an eaglelike nose, his mouth open. He looked dead.

"Okay. I've seen him. Let's go." Park stooped down again below the level of the sill.

She smiled up at him. "You 'fraid," she said.

"What is there to be afraid of? I just think we'd better get back to work."

She followed him out of the yard and back around to the vegetable garden, grinning like a jack-o'-lantern.

If he didn't appear on the porch at three thirty, Frank would know that something was wrong. As it turned out, "Missed you at milking this morning" was all Frank said that might mean he thought anything was wrong.

"Sorry." Park mumbled something about oversleeping, to which Frank simply nodded, got the key from the drawer, and, supplied with gun and ammunition, they started out.

Would it show? Would Park shake so much that he wouldn't be able to get near the target and Frank would suspect . . . but, miraculously, he did about as well as he had the day before.

"You're getting the hang of it," Frank said when Park managed to get two fives within four shots of each other. Frank cleared his throat. Now it was coming. Park, on his stomach with the gun on his shoulder, froze in position. "I know you're wondering why I don't just take you in to introduce you to the Colonel." He sighed, and so, more quietly, did Park. "I, well, I never—I never know how things will affect him. You never can be sure. The first stroke—it was a mild one, but it came right after the divorce, and this last one . . ."

"Divorce?"

Frank stooped down so his head was just higher than

Park's. "I'm sorry," he said. "Am I talking out of turn? I just assumed your mother had told you."

"Told me what?" He could hardly get the words out.

"You didn't know that she divorced Park?"

Park's throat closed up. He couldn't have answered if his life depended on it. Divorce? The idea had never crossed his mind. When? Why? And why hadn't she told him? Didn't he have a right to know something like that?

"I'm sorry," Frank said again, this time more softly. "You shouldn't have heard it this way."

It explained some things, anyhow. If she had divorced his father before his death, then she would feel different about his dying, wouldn't she? Maybe guilty. Maybe she *was* guilty.

"You okay?" Frank had asked it. See—it was her fault, not his. Frank had said right out, *You okay?* That was exactly the sign he'd asked God for, wasn't it? Well, not exactly, but close, close. Divorced? How could you be both dead and divorced? If your husband was dead, didn't that cancel out the divorce? Or was it the other way around? His head was hot and muddled.

"You ready to start back?" Frank was studying him anxiously. "I'm really sorry, son. It wasn't up to me—I shouldn't have been the one—"

Park was standing now, concentrating on unloading the gun. He had lost heart for the final shot. He didn't even belong to this place. He was divorced. He didn't have a father anymore—even a dead father. It wasn't his grandfather or uncle or farm. His mother had seen to that. What was he doing here, anyhow? No wonder they'd treated him so funny. He didn't belong here at all. They were just being nice to let him come. They hadn't wanted him. They weren't even kin anymore.

"You okay?" Frank asked again.

He nodded and handed the gun and shell back to Frank and climbed into the jeep. What was he supposed to do?

Frank put the ammo box and gun in the back of the jeep. Without talking, he carried the target to the barn. He got in and started the motor before he looked at Park again. Then it was a quick glance as he turned to see where he was backing. He shifted gears and cleared his throat as though he was going to speak again, but he didn't. He just roared forward and, bouncing more than usual, headed for the house.

Park lay awake, straining for the sound. The old house was full of noises. He could hear the *chuck chuck chuck chuck* of the grandfather clock in the downstairs hallway, the muffled, sleepy sounds of the cows, and the occasional bleat of a calf. Further away, the throaty complaints of sheep and the cranking of truck gears on the highway ramp, the swish of traffic on the interstate. Once he thought he heard a creak, as though someone were walking the night house, but it was gone, no matter how he strained.

What would he do if he heard the sound? Go down and stare at the old man again? Run the risk of running away another time? Try to talk to him? Upset him once more? Probably cause another stroke? He tossed over and grabbed the covers more tightly around him. What was he supposed to do? Maybe Frank had been trying to tell him when he let that slip about the divorce. Maybe he'd missed what he needed desperately to know by going to pieces over the stinking divorce.

But divorce? She'd shut the golden airman out of their lives on purpose. How could she do that? Park tried to conjure up his father's face. He concentrated on the snapshot, but all he could see was the tilt of the head and the angle of the cap; the face was blurred, out of focus. He squeezed his eyes together and tried to see his father's name in the black granite. He raised his right hand in the darkness and tried to feel the warmth of the stone, tried to recapture those few minutes of his life when his father had been real to him. His whole body shook with the sobs that would not come.

THE KING GOES RIDING

·11·

Splat. Something cold and wet had hit his face, startling him out of sleep. Of course, there she stood again beside the bed, so short her chin just cleared the pillow on the high bed. "Up!" she commanded.

In reply he slung the wet washcloth at her nose, but she dodged it nimbly. "Frank say come milk."

"I'm coming. Now out! Out!"

"I wait," she said prissily. "You sleep more."

"I'm awake. I can't get dressed until you get yourself out of here, for cripes' sake."

Her eyes danced with mischief. "Why?"

"Get out of here. I mean it, and take that filthy washrag with you."

She stood still for a minute more, obviously enjoying the tease, and then she turned and walked out, leaving the cloth on the floor and the door wide open. He jumped out of the bed and in two more leaps had pitched out the washcloth and slammed the door after it. Cripes. He was covered with sweat, though the early morning air was as cool as ever, and his clothes seemed to stick as he tried to pull them on. At last he was ready. He took a deep breath and blew it out, trying to get himself under control before he opened the door.

She was gone, but the stupid washrag lay there grinning at him. He stepped on it as he went downstairs.

Frank was so patient with him that Park thought he might scream. He wasn't sure which was worse, the sassiness of the girl or the quiet, unhurried, repeated instructions of the man. Both said to Park—you fool, you idiot, you know-nothing.

You have disgraced the knightly code. Henceforth, the sword that your father wore can no longer hang at your side, and since you have proved yourself unworthy of the noble device upon your shield, you may no longer carry that shield. And without sword or shield, what need have you for lance or armor? Go, you foul and loathsome creature who hast besmirched the very image of knighthood. Go and wander in the alien wilderness far from the world of gentleness and honor, stripped of every semblance of your past nobility—

I'll go home today. The thought occurred to him in the middle of a squeeze-pull. There was no reason to stick around. They didn't want him. He upset the old man. He didn't belong here. It was very simple. Park was suddenly quite calm. *I can walk to town. It's not much further than the distance to the Metro stop at home, and I haven't all that much to carry. I'll just walk into town and catch the next bus to D.C. There's bound to be one every hour or so.*

"He's gone."

"But why? Why? Why would he leave without so much as a good-bye? We never thanked him."

"He never waits for thanks. Surely you know that. He is a hermit. Legend has it that he was once the noblest of all the knights of the Round Table, but because of some grievous sin . . ."

"Yet surely he has done penance long since for his error."

"Ah, more than penance, and yet he wanders still, doing acts of mercy—"

"I want you to meet the Colonel today," Frank was saying in his quiet voice from behind the next cow.

"What?" Park jumped so that his cow lifted a hind foot and nearly knocked over the pail. Park grabbed for it. "What?"

"I've been thinking it over," Frank continued. "It may upset him a little, but in the long run, he needs to see you. I was wrong to put it off."

Haaaa. "It's okay, really." Park broke out in a sweat. "I don't want to bother him. He doesn't know me from Adam. It wouldn't be right."

"Well, he ought to know you. You're his grandson—his namesake."

"But I'm divorced. You said so."

Frank gave a little laugh, then immediately sobered. "*You're* not divorced. Your parents were divorced."

Park stiffened. Frank shouldn't make fun of him. "I know. But it *is* different."

"Only because your mother chose— Look, I'm not judging her. She had her reasons. But that doesn't make you less a member of this family."

You could've fooled me, Park thought, but he kept his mouth shut.

"I haven't been much help, I know."

"It's okay," Park said tightly. Just don't laugh at me, okay? Frank got up and took his bucket into the separator room. When he came back in, he stopped first beside Park. "I'll come up to the house right after breakfast."

"No! I mean, I don't want to upset him."

Frank put his hand on Park's shoulder. If he noticed how much the boy was trembling, he gave no sign. "Don't worry, it's going to be okay," he said.

There was no mistaking it. Frank had said the words. A day late, but *It's going to be okay*. So. What did God mean? Frank didn't say *It is okay*; he said, *It's going to be okay*. So what did God mean? That Park should be patient? That he shouldn't leave today after all? That he should let Frank take him in and see the old man? *Haaaa*. He couldn't. He couldn't walk in there and look into those eyes again.

He raced up to his room as soon as milking was done and began to throw his clothes into his suitcase. It was a small canvas bag, and with everything pitched in, Park couldn't force the zipper around, so he had to take everything out and fold each piece. His hands were shaking. What should he do about his sneakers? He couldn't wear them on the bus. Not with their large green stains and still smelling. He'd have to wear his leather shoes, even if they did hurt his feet. He looked around the room for a newspaper or brown bag, but there was no sign of ordinary living in the room except for his open suitcase. No stack of old shopping bags or papers as there would have been at home. Maybe in the kitchen, surely on the back porch—

"Where you go?"

He wheeled around to see Thanh in the doorway. "Can't you knock before you come busting in?"

She grinned impishly and knocked on the already opened door. "Okay now, Mister Cool Head?"

"No. What do you want?"

"Frank say you come now."

"I'm busy."

Her eyes widened in fake innocence. "But you meet old grandfather. Frank say."

"Geek." He muttered the word under his breath.

"What?"

He ignored her. What was he to do? He couldn't go in there. Those eyes fiery with pain—that *haaaa*.

"You 'fraid."

"No." He stuck his sneakers on and, without stopping to retie them, pushed past her and went down the hall and to the stairs. Frank stood at the bottom, smiling up at him. There was no escape.

"Morning," said Frank, just as though he hadn't seen him all day or something. "Look, I've got him in his chair. I thought maybe you'd like to push him out to the front porch. It's a nice, warm day, and it would be good for him to get some fresh air. All right?"

Park nodded and took a deep breath. Then he followed Frank to the door of the old man's room.

"Colonel?"

The old man sat hunched in a wheelchair. He was wearing a navy blue flannel bathrobe over gray pajamas and had a multicolored afghan on his lap and tucked around his knees. His head turned slightly upward at a funny angle toward where Frank stood. "I've brought the boy in to see you. Park's son."

Park froze, waiting for the old man's cry, but it didn't come. It was as though the old man didn't see, didn't understand. His eyes had gone dull, and the thin fingers of his left hand stroked the afghan in a weak, useless gesture.

"Your grandson"—Park wished Frank would tone it down—"your grandson here is going to wheel you out on the porch so you can get some sun while you visit. All right?" There was no reply, not a nod or an eyeblink. Maybe—did he dare hope? Maybe the old man couldn't remember seeing him before. Anyhow, his grandfather was not upset or crazy at the sight of him. Frank motioned for Park to come closer.

Park took a baby step across the threshold. What was he supposed to do? Speak? Shake the dead-looking puffy right hand? Kiss the wrinkled cheek? Park gave a tiny shudder. "Hello." It was more a squeak than a greeting. The old man gave no sign of recognition.

Frank smiled over the invalid's head. "Come around here. Just remember at the doors to tilt a bit so the wheels can get over the sills."

Pushing the chair was easy. The old man seemed to weigh very little. Frank went ahead, opened and held the front door, and then showed Park where to place the chair and how to fix the brake. His uncle knelt and tucked the afghan more securely under the old man's hips and around his legs and feet, as though it were winter instead of a bright summer morning. "There," he said, smiling up into the old face before getting up from his knees. He leaned over and gave the old man's knees a pat. "Little Park will take good care of you.

He can tell you all about himself, and if you need anything, you just let him know."

How was this old man supposed to let anyone know anything? As far as Park could see, he couldn't even gesture, much less talk. Park waited until Frank crossed the yard and headed for his own house; then he backed himself over to the porch swing and sat down. From there he could study the old man's profile—his beaked nose and balding head, his hunched shoulders, his thin left hand fingering the bright blues and oranges and greens of the afghan.

He can tell you all about himself. Should Park try to talk? How could he talk? His mouth was dry as day-old toast, his nose slick with sweat. He took off his glasses and wiped his face on the tail of his T-shirt. As he hooked the frames back over his ears, he was suddenly aware of birds. He listened. He could hear them everywhere, but he couldn't see them. He stared at the big maple tree nearest the porch. Occasionally, if he watched closely, he could see a flash of wings. There were no cars on the road running past the farm, but he could hear faint sounds of traffic from the interstate if he concentrated, though the chattering of the birds and occasional lowing of the cows and baaing of sheep drowned out the sounds of men and machines. Heavy, he felt very heavy. In the far distance a phone was ringing. He was dimly aware of the muffled sound of conversation through the walls. His head began to droop, but he jerked himself awake.

Was the man nodding? Park couldn't tell. If the sick man fell asleep, would he fall out of his chair? Then what?

A board creaked behind the swing. He spun around to see Thanh tiptoeing up behind him. "Oh," she said. "You see." Disappointed to be caught.

"Yes, I see," he said through his clenched teeth. "What are you doing here?"

"I want see old grandfather," she whispered, as though they were co-conspirators.

"Get off the freaking porch and go home to your mother."

She tossed her hair. "Can't."

"You most certainly can."

"Can't. Baby come."

"Now?" He had forgotten to whisper.

She shrugged. "They go hospital now."

As she spoke, Park heard the sound of a motor starting. Then he saw the pickup backing and turning to go out of the driveway of the house below the garden and onto the road. He stood up to watch until it went around the bend and out of sight. He was surprised to feel his heart speeding up. Why should he be excited? Or was it fear?

Thanh was watching him closely. He sat down, waiting for a teasing remark, but instead she said, "I not care." Her shoulder was hunched up and her little jaw tight and straight. "I not!" she insisted, as though he had expressed doubt. "Not even if boy!"

"No?" He rocked back on his heels to put the swing in motion. The little geek. Who did she think she was fooling? He stared at his feet—part dirty white, part green—toe, heel, toe—then gave a harder shove. He lifted his feet off the porch floor. The chains of the swing creaked rhythmically. He wanted to shove harder to keep the motion going, but Thanh was in the way. "Move."

"No."

"Aren't you supposed to be working or something?"

"You not work."

"I'm—" What was he doing? "I'm taking care of him."

She shrugged and made her way around the end of the swing past the old man and into the house. He heard her say something to Mrs. Davenport and then, faintly, the sound of the back screen door. He was glad she was gone. He could almost pretend he was alone. A guilty glance at the old man. He didn't seem to have changed position. Just the restless picking at the afghan to prove that he wasn't a wax figure. Does he know what's going on? Can he hear what we say? If hearing about me upset him, why isn't he upset now? Are his eyes closed? Park bent forward. Yes, his head was nodding. He was falling asleep. Park dragged the swing to a stop with his heels. He didn't want to risk waking the old man.

He yawned. Maybe while the old man was asleep— He lay down and pulled his feet up on the swing. It wasn't long enough for him to stretch out. He lay there with his knees bent, the swing moving ever so slightly. There was a heavy scent of flowers, and bees hummed a few feet from his head. Far away on the interstate ramp, a truck shifted gears.

Where was he? The narrow boards were hard on the back of his head. He was swaying, and the ceiling above him was slightly blistered with peeling gray paint. He sat up. He had no idea how long he'd been asleep. Or maybe he hadn't slept at all. Or—

The wheelchair was gone. Park jumped up and ran into the house, down the hall. The bedroom door stood open. The room was empty.

He opened the dining room door to call Mrs. Davenport, but as he looked toward the kitchen, he stopped dead. He could see Mrs. Davenport in the kitchen rocker, her head back, her eyes closed, her mouth slightly open. Her knitting lay sprawled across her wide lap. Thanh. It was Thanh who had taken the old man away.

He searched the front yard, panic mounting. Jupe came to meet him, but there was no wheelchair, no old man. Wheelchairs didn't just disappear. He flew around to the back. Oh, God, what had that crazy kid done?

He ran for the back gate—"Stay!" he commanded a startled Jupe—down the path, around the chicken house. That was when he saw them. Racing down the hill. She had the wheelchair tilted on the back wheels and was either pushing it or holding on for dear life, he couldn't tell. She was already past the barnyard gate, which was swung wide open against the side of the shed, and on the final slope, heading pell-mell for the springhouse, her hair flying out behind.

"Stop!" he screamed as he ran, not caring what he stepped on or in. She'd kill him, and it would all be Park's fault. "Stop, you fool, stop!"

Whether she couldn't or wouldn't, at any rate, she slowed not at all until she came to an abrupt halt at the door of the springhouse.

The afghan had come loose and was sliding off the old man's lap, but his one good hand was clutching the arm of the chair so tightly that the purple veins looked near to bursting. Park caught up then, panting, his heart half out of his body.

"I can't believe you! You fool! You stupid fool. You could have killed him!"

"He like," she said, her head tilted, her jaw set.

Park looked full into the old man's face. The mouth was twisted strangely to one side, the eyes bright. God in heaven. He was. The old man was smiling.

A CONFUSION OF CROWS

·12·

Park might as well have been a cinder block. He stood there, gray and cold, while the girl retucked the afghan, opened the springhouse door, and maneuvered the chair partway inside. She filled the coconut shell with water and held it to the old man's lips. "Here," she commanded, "you drink." He bent to the shell and took a long swallow. When he lifted his head, water was trickling from the corner of his mouth. Deliberately, he licked his lips. The crooked smile reappeared.

"More?" she asked.

Park couldn't determine how she knew the old man's answer, or if indeed she did, but she held the shell to his mouth again, and he took another long drink. "Okay?" she asked, patting his wet face with her shirttail. Again Park couldn't see any answer, but she was satisfied, so she backed the chair out of the door and turned it around.

"Now," she said to Park, who was still standing block-bodied outside the door. "You push back. I push all way here."

The road was steep and dirt-rutted, pocked with small stones and booby-trapped with cow piles. The wheels kept catching on a stone or in a rut, and Park strained to get the weight of man (no longer did he seem light) and chair over even the smallest hump. Thanh skipped ahead and grinned at him. "Oooo, so hard for big boy. Not so Superman, yes?"

Geek. "You gotta help me," he said, nodding at the gaping gate, wondering how she'd opened it on the way down.

"I do before," she explained, reading his mind. "He like long ride, yes, Mister Grandfather?" She ducked her head down to get the old man's assent. "See," she said. "He say 'Like.' "

Something exploded in Park's chest. He couldn't let himself think what might have happened. "Just close it, okay?"

She smirked and danced about, not moving toward the gate, even after he'd pushed his way well past it.

"We got to get him back before Mrs. Davenport—before Frank—"

He'd invoked the magic name. Thanh skipped back, closed, and fastened the gate. He was relieved, grateful, but he wasn't about to say so. After all, who had gotten them into this mess? Suppose—he couldn't suppress the picture of the old man flying out of the chair, landing in a crumpled tangle of afghan and bathrobe on the dirty road. Oh, God. Sweat was pouring out from under his hair, sending his glasses slithering down his nose. He banged them back in place with one hand.

Park took the low road near the barns, keeping as far away from the house as possible. If he could get the old man back onto the porch without the housekeeper knowing . . . He was hardly breathing as they rounded the road and started toward the main gate. If they went until the barn road met the road going up to the front of the house, it would be easier pushing. The shortcut up the grassy hillside would be torture. Park kept glancing back at the house. So far, so good.

At the fork he turned the chair and started up the drive to the house. Behind him he could hear a car approaching on the road. If Frank should come home—but it wasn't Frank. The sound of the motor passed the gate and faded over the next hill.

"Hurry," he commanded in a mixture of anxiety and relief, "get the gate."

"You so big boy. You do."

He mustn't lose his temper. "I need help," he said evenly. Out of the side of his eye, he could see her satisfied smile. The geek. She wasn't scared, much less sorry. She'd be perfectly willing for everyone to think *he* was the one who had taken the old man off the porch.

Thanh! Me? I small girl. I no push big chair! Her eyes would be round with astonished innocence.

Jupe was waiting in the yard, tail wagging. "Please," Park said. That seemed to mollify her, so she opened the gate. Jupe slipped out and put his nose on the old man's lap. To Park's amazement, the clawlike left hand slid over and touched the dog's head.

But Park couldn't wait. "Sorry," he muttered to man or dog and pushed the chair forward. He managed, even though he had to navigate the low step up from the walk to the porch. He strained until he could feel a tight band of pain across his forehead. At last he got the back wheels safely onto the porch and pushed the chair to the place Frank had put it earlier. Then he set the brake and fell exhausted onto the swing.

Thanh had disappeared. Coward. Jupe came over again to nuzzle the afghan. This time the old man made no attempt to pat him. The left hand was moving in an agitated manner. The eyes were wilder. He opened his mouth as wide as his paralysis would allow, but before he could make the terrible sound, Park fled to the kitchen.

Mrs. Davenport was still sprawled back in the rocker. The knitting had slipped onto the floor.

"Uh—" Park began. She jumped up straight. "I think he—" Park waved in the direction of the porch. "I think he wants to come inside."

"Well." She searched her lap, then her surroundings for her knitting, swooped it up from the floor, and jabbed a needle into the next stitch. "You're a big, strong boy. You ought to be able to push him to his room while I finish this row." She was knitting furiously.

"Can't," he said. "I gotta—gotta go to the bathroom." Where he stayed hidden until he was sure the porch and hall were clear.

It was noon, and Frank had not come back from the hospital. Mrs. Davenport telephoned the garden house to summon Thanh to lunch. There was no answer.

"Oh, that girl. Never mind. If she gets hungry, she'll come. You'd think she'd care. Poor Frank. That woman's scared to death of an American hospital, so he thinks he can't leave her alone. You'd think the girl would want to make life easier for him. He's spoiled her, if you ask me. Not that anyone does."

Park said nothing, concentrating instead on chewing every bite sixty times. Mr. Campanelli at home insisted that chewing every bite sixty times was responsible for his long life. Park didn't believe it, but when you had to count chews, you couldn't worry about much else, even taste.

Why would you want to live to old age if you were crippled or paralyzed or—*haaaa*—living under a curse? He champed harder on the tough chicken. Curse. Or disgrace. You shouldn't just give in. Why should a disgraced knight become a hermit? He should do like the Japanese samurai did. They didn't just wither up into monks when things went wrong. If they got kicked out, they turned into rogue warriors and went about making their own rules, fighting for themselves.

"Are you listening to me, sonny?"

"Huh? I mean, excuse me?"

"Did our little patient just sleep the morning away?"

"Uh. Yeah. Yes. Yes, ma'am."

She shook her head. "We'd be better off dead, wouldn't we? Poor old thing. Well, one of these days we'll have a big one that will just carry us off to a better land." She stood up and began clearing the kitchen table. "None too soon, if you ask me. None too soon."

"I'll wash," Park said to make her shut up.

"Well, fine." She put down her stack of dishes and wiped off her hands. "Fine. That's a sweet boy. We'll just go down the hall and see if we—he needs anything before my little afternoon break. Thank you. That's very nice."

The keys were there in the back of the drawer nearest the sink. He pocketed them quickly and then did the dishes.

Later, when he was sure she had gone upstairs to her own room and closed the door, he crept onto the back porch and got the gun.

It was a long walk to the far pasture. Park was tired from the events of the morning; still, he was feeling better than he had all day. For once in his life, he was taking charge. He dragged the bale of hay with the target attached out of the barn and set it on the low stump and stretched out on his stomach facing it.

The sheep, who had moved slightly away as he had come into the pasture, turned now to stare at him. He remembered hearing that sheep were about the most stupid animal in God's creation, but they didn't look stupid. They looked very wise, very knowing, staring down their long noses at him. Stupid boy, who do you think you are?

"Shoo," he said, waving an arm in their direction. "Git!" The sheep jostled a few yards to the left, then turned again to stare. He gave his attention to the gun. Let them watch. He didn't care. He pressed the walnut stock hard into his shoulder, released the safety. With his jaw set, he squinted his left eye and took a careful sighting on the bull's-eye. He squeezed the trigger. There was a weak *click*. He tried again. Again the ineffectual *click*. He'd forgotten to load.

Maaaa, said a large ewe through her elegant nose. He scrunched up on his knees so he could get the box of shells out of his jeans pocket. The stupid sheep stood staring at him with her mouth half open. He turned his back on her while he loaded. When he stretched out again, she had lost interest.

Once more he released the safety, took careful aim, and shot, but his hands were shaking. The bullet missed the target by several feet. At the *plack* of the rifle, the sheep lifted their heads and, in a body, galumphed over the hill and out of sight. He waited until the clatter of their bells was reduced to an occasional hollow clank before he reloaded.

It was very still. He could hear the buzz of insects in the grass. He kept motionless, the gun pressed against his shoulder, as though he were drawing strength from the wood. He let the quiet of the afternoon seep into his tightly clenched body. It was a long time since he'd felt so at peace.

Just then a flock of crows broke the stillness, arguing their way down to the earth, squabbling over something one of them had found protruding from the bale behind the target. He sighted down the barrel. What huge birds they were. And so sure of themselves. The joint chiefs of staff in furious discussion, each convinced that he alone knew the answer.

"Noooo!" Out of nowhere. She flung herself on his back and grabbed at his arm. The gun went off. There was a scraping and crashing and cawing. The crows flew up in angry confusion.

All but one. "You kill!" Thanh screamed, jumping off his back and running across to the fallen bird. "You kill! You murder!"

Park struggled to his feet. It was not possible. He could hardly hit a three-foot target. How could he kill a crow with a single shot from an ancient twenty-two? It was her fault. She had jumped on his back and grabbed his arm. He had had no intention of shooting at the birds. He hadn't. He was sure he hadn't.

"Come," she ordered, her voice shaking. "See what you do, murder."

He paused to check the chamber, though he knew all too well the gun was empty before he laid it on the grass.

"I say, come." She began to sob with anger.

He stumbled across to where she stood. The crow lay behind the bale, sprawled crazily on its back, its wings spread in surrender. The head was twisted against its right wing, so that its left eye stared up wide and angry. Where had he seen that look? *Haaaa* . . .

What had he done? Killing was too easy. It shouldn't be easy. You did it without even meaning to, and there was no way to take it back.

Tears started in his eyes. She mustn't see him cry. He turned away to wipe his face; then, just as he was taking off his glasses, she hurled herself against his back and knocked him hard onto the sharp, stubbly grass. She had his body pinned, and she was pummeling his back, crying and screaming, "You murder! You murder! You no good murder!"

He struggled to get up. He was stronger than she, but he couldn't shake her off. When he managed to turn enough to grab her right arm, she leaned forward and sank her teeth deep into his wrist. He yelled out in pain.

"So!" she cried. "Now you feel!" She bent to bite him again. He let go her arm and rolled hard to throw her off. Before he could stand up, she was on his chest. He smacked her across the face.

"So! Now you beat up girl! You no good."

"You bit me, you little geek. You bite me again and you'll know what beating up is." He grabbed both her wrists and squeezed tight. "You just better pray you didn't break my glasses."

With a quick twist in and down against his thumbs, she was free. He could see the contempt in her eyes. Slowly she got up.

"I let you go now," she said. "Even you murder, you nothing." She spit on the ground just beside his left shoulder. "I no fight nothing." She picked up his glasses and threw them at him and then picked up her cap and crammed it on her head.

She was right. His fury at her trickled coldly into despair. He put his glasses on. They were hardly bent. She was right. For all his proud dreams, he had proved himself nothing. He waited until she had walked away over the hill and out of sight before he got to his feet.

The crow. He'd have to bury it or hide it or something. He couldn't just leave it in the middle of the pasture with a bullet hole in its—

He forced himself to walk over again to where the crow lay. There was no blood to be seen. Birds bled, didn't they? Of course they bled. Where was the blood? He nudged the body gently with the green toe of his sneaker.

Then he saw the blood. Not much, just a little where the bird's foot should have been.

Poor bird. It seemed more horrible somehow to die by having your foot shot off than by being killed cleanly through the heart. It was a stupid, senseless way to die. I'm really sorry, he said to the crow. I didn't mean to. I swear I didn't.

Wait. Did he imagine it? Another gentle nudge. There. He stopped breathing. There. He was sure he saw—yes. Yes. It was stirring. Not much, but definitely moving. He hadn't killed it.

It was a sign, a sign from heaven. God was saying "okay." Everything would be all right.

"Thanh!" he yelled. "Come back! Come back! It's alive!"

OTHER SIDE OF THE DARK

·13·

She didn't come back. Perhaps she couldn't hear him. Never mind. He would tell her, but first he must find a safe place for the crow. He took off his T-shirt and laid it on the ground. The bird cocked its head toward Park and tried weakly to peck him. Carefully Park put his hands underneath its body and slid it over onto his shirt. Then he wrapped the shirt about the bird and began to carry it gently to the barn.

The crow was reviving under his hands, pecking him harder and harder through his shirt. "That's it, girl. That's it. Keep fighting. Ow!"

The crow continued to struggle, but he would not let it go, digging with his elbows and forearms into the hay and climbing as high as he could up into the stacks of bales in the old barn. He laid the crow, T-shirt and all, upon the highest bale he could reach.

"Okay?" he asked the angry, piercing eyes. "You going to be all right?" He reached up, meaning to release the crow from the flaps of the shirt but jerked back quickly from the now powerful beak. "I'll be right back," he promised. "I'm going to get help."

"No," said Mrs. Davenport. "Mr. Frank called and said he'd come back to milk, but I don't think we'll see him before then. Why?"

"Uh. Nothing." Mrs. Davenport was not the person to tell about the crow or the gun. "You haven't seen Thanh?"

"No, I haven't, and we're not very pleased with that young lady, either. She's got Mr. Frank all worried." She seemed to see Park suddenly. "Where is our shirt?"

"Hot," he said, smiling weakly. "Hot as—real hot out there. How 'bout if I find Thanh for you?"

"What a nice boy. We called her and phoned Frank's house. No answer at all."

She was not in the springhouse. He tried the barns, calling and crawling over the hay in the lofts. *Pssst. Pssssssst!* He jumped back. The cat was arched, ready to claw his face if he came any closer to her nest of kittens. "Sorry," he mumbled, then smiled to himself for apologizing to a cat.

She didn't seem to be in either barn, so he went to the little house beyond the garden. She might be home, not answering the telephone. The more he thought about it, the more likely it seemed that she wouldn't answer the phone. Any news it brought would sound bad to her.

The house was boxlike, with aluminum siding—one floor, not even a real porch, more a covered stoop at the front door. A farmhand's house. Park knocked. No answer. He knocked again. Not that she was apt to come to the door if she wouldn't answer the telephone. He knocked once more, then tried the knob.

It was cool inside the house, and dark. The shades had all been drawn against the summer sun. "Thanh?" The living room was overcrowded with heavy old furniture that must have come down from the big house. One wall was lined to the ceiling with a bookcase, which was packed as densely as a commuter train. Except for the books, the house felt deserted. It was so quiet he could hear the ticking of an unseen clock. He took another step forward into the room. "Thanh? It's me, Park."

Still no answer. He listened intently. She might be watching him right this minute, for all he knew. The house smelled peculiar. It was a smell he knew from somewhere. Then he remembered. The refugees who had lived in his apartment house a few years back. Their cooking had stunk up the whole building. It was some kind of fish sauce.

He moved across the room to a swinging door at the left back wall and pushed it open a crack. The smell was even stronger. The kitchen. Except for the odor, it was neat as a pin. He wondered how Frank stood the smell. Did he eat that food? He let the kitchen door swing back. He had no time to waste in speculation.

A second door opened into a narrow hallway. Looking down the length of it, he saw two doors on either side, all closed. "Thanh?" he called again. "It's me. I need your help." Surely if he sounded humble . . .

Still no answer. He tried the first door to his right. It was a closet. The one on the left was a bathroom. He went down the hall, feeling for all the world like a burglar. If only she'd answer. The house was spooking him.

He turned the knob of the second door on the right. It was a small bedroom clogged with a high double bed, a large mahogany dresser, a baby crib, a small dresser, and a changing table. He closed the door again. Thanh was not likely to be hiding among the baby things.

There was only one door left. It had to be hers. He knocked. No answer. "Thanh?" He cracked open the door. "You in there? I got something I have to tell you. About the bird." Still no answer. He took a step in. A narrow single bed protruded from the wall at his right. Its white counterpane fell starched and wrinkleless to the floor. To the right of the bed was a tiny bedside table; to the left was a small maple dresser with a bleached white crocheted runner. The room was almost painfully neat, with only a stuffed brown bear on the bed to suggest that it belonged to a child. But even the bear reminded him of something sad he couldn't quite remember. And, yes, on the bedside table was a funny, old-fashioned-looking child's lamp. He walked around the length of the bed to examine it. A Humpty-Dumpty night-light with a reading light at the top. Weird. Probably fetch a lot of money at one of those fancy little junk/antique shops at home.

Then he saw what the belly of Humpty-Dumpty had concealed from the doorway—a small framed picture. Not a blurred snapshot, but one taken in a cheap studio with a painted-in background of mountains and trees. And in the center a couple, a smiling young woman with Thanh's face but fuller and happier, and, with his arm around her, a laughing, dark-haired airman with his cap set at a jaunty angle.

Trembling, Park reached for it. But just as he picked it up, a hand shot out from under the bed and grabbed his ankle. He went crashing painfully to the floor. His glasses stayed on his nose, but the picture flew out of his hand and landed facedown with an ominous cracking sound.

Her head came out from under the starched counterpane. "What you do here?" she demanded.

"What are *you* doing here?"

"My room," she said. Then she saw the picture. She slid out from under the bed and snatched it up. There was a long crack from the woods in the lower corner to the mountains in the top, right through the bodies of the happy couple, who smiled on as though nothing had happened. "Thanh picture!" she cried. "You break. You murder."

"It's just the glass," he said. "I'll get you a new glass."

She was swaying back and forth on her haunches, hugging the picture to her chest. "You murder." She was crying. "You kill bird. Now Thanh picture."

He had to be careful. He was very close, and if he frightened her or angered her—

"Thanh," he said gently, his voice quavering. "Who is that man in your picture?"

She hugged it more tightly. "Not business of you." If only it weren't.

He tried again, forcing the words through the glacier that had moved up from his chest into his throat. "Where did you get the picture? Please?"

"I no steal."

"Of course not. Did your mother, or Frank—?"

"Not Frank," she said angrily. "Frank not like. He no say. Thanh know." She smiled a little, as though at the moment she liked the idea of displeasing Frank.

"Please tell me about the picture." He was begging, which was the wrong tactic with Thanh, and he knew it. Still, what was he to do?

"No," she said. "You murder."

133

"I didn't kill the bird," he said humbly. "That's what I came to tell you. It's not dead, but we have to take care of it. It's hurt."

She cut her eyes at him suspiciously. "What you say?"

"I put him up in the barn. On my shirt." He glanced at his bare chest. It was evidence, wasn't it, that he wasn't lying? "Then I came to get you."

"You no lie?"

He raised his right hand. "I swear."

She got up and put the picture down, running her finger across the crack as if to smooth it away, straightening it to make sure it was back in exactly its proper position. "Why you sit like fat rock? Hurry!"

They ran. She was faster than he and scrambled over the lower gate like a monkey, but his awkwardness no longer mattered. When they got as far as the springhouse, he was out of breath and grateful that she swung down toward it. "Wait," she commanded. He stood panting outside the door while she went inside. She emerged carrying the coconut shell half full of water. "He need," she said, and because she was carrying the water, they walked the rest of the way to the far pasture.

The crow watched them suspiciously as they climbed up the steps made by the bales of hay. "Aw right, baby," she crooned. "Aw right. We bring water. See?" She ripped hay from the bale in front of the bird and nestled the coconut shell into the depression, her small hands darting in and out in an exotic dance, evading the jabs of the angry beak.

"Drink. Drink," she said. "Good. Good." The bird paused in its frantic attack, lifted its head, and stared at her. The children stood motionless, holding their breath. At last the crow moved its shining black neck over the shell, dipped in, and lifted its head to swallow. "Good baby," Thanh crooned. "Good. Good."

They did not move as the bird dipped into the shell three or four more times and then shifted, settling its beak into its breast. "Aw right," Thanh whispered. "Go sleep now."

A tightness began to loosen in his chest. He stretched out his fingers to touch the ebony feathers.

"No touch," she warned softly, catching his arm in her cool hand. "He might hurt you."

He nodded, swallowing hard.

She let go his arm and slipped her hand in quickly to retrieve the shell. Without a word, they climbed down and left the barn. She was smiling at Park. "He not kill," she said.

"No," Park answered and smiled back.

"Tonight we bring food, more water."

Park nodded. At the springhouse, they went in. She dipped the shell and held it up solemnly for him to drink, and then, without wiping the lip of the shell, she drank as well. It seemed the right moment.

"Thanh."

"Yeah?"

"Your picture. Is that your father?"

"Why you ask my father?"

"Because I think—that man—that man in the picture is my father."

She looked at him over the rim of the coconut shell, puzzled. "What name father?" she asked.

"Park. Parkington Waddell Broughton the Fourth."

She sat down on the edge of the trough. "Father name that?"

"Yes," he said, sitting down beside her. "My father. They didn't tell you his name? Your father?"

"Just name 'Father.' " She was shaking her head. "Mother alway say, 'Someday, someday. Tell Thanh someday.' But don't tell nothing. Say now Frank father. But alway I keep picture. In Saigon. On boat. Even nothing to eat. No water. Even guns shoot. Two, three year in camp. Alway, alway from baby time I keep picture. Someday I find, I think." Her face clouded, but she didn't cry. She was tough, like his mother.

My life closed twice before its close. His mother knew. Park shivered. She had known all along. This little brown girl with stringy, sweaty hair under her jaunty little red cap—she was the closing—the cause for his mother's angry grief, which had festered unhealing all these years. He had thought it was death that could not be forgiven, and all the time it had been life.

"He's dead," Park said softly.

The girl nodded her head, her eyes fixed on the patched knees of her jeans. "I think so maybe. I say, okay, Thanh, new country, new father. But," her voice quavered, "but Frank have baby. Maybe boy. Don't want silly girl—silly girl, not even own." She gave a long, shuddering sigh.

They sat there quietly in the cool dark of the springhouse, their bodies touching lightly. He wished Randy could meet her. Maybe— Suddenly she twisted around to look at him. "What you say your father? In Thanh picture, your father?"

"Yes. I think so." He stared into the little brown face, the bright, mischievous eyes, the stupid baseball cap cocked at exactly the same familiar angle. "I'm sure," he said. "You can ask Frank, but I'm sure we have the same father."

She stood up, one hand propped on her small hip, the other still holding the shell. "Then I have bruzzuh already. Not worry baby. I have big fat fool bruzzuh all life."

"That's what I was trying to tell you."

"We bruzzuh. You, me?" She looked down at him. "Crazy thing I ever hear." She shook her head, unbelieving.

"I swear," he said. "I couldn't believe it either. But I know—I'm sure."

"And we have same old grandfahzuh?"

"And same crow."

"You crazy," she said, pouring out the rest of the water on his head. The cold water felt good running down his hot neck. "Oh, my good," she said. "I forget milk. We better go. Frank kill us sure."

"Thanh." He pulled the gun-cabinet keys from his pocket. "The gun. I gotta go back. It's still in the pasture."

"No worry, bruzzuh. Later. You and me fix. Frank not know nothing." She flung out her little hand, dismissing all his cares.

THE COMPANY OF THE GRAIL

·14·

Frank was already milking. Thanh put her finger to her lips and motioned for Park to follow her into the separator room. She was creeping in on tiptoe, her rubber sandals flapping from her little brown heels. She pointed for him to get a stool and bucket as she got her own, and, still tiptoeing, led the way into the barn.

"You don't have to sneak in," Frank said. "I already noticed you weren't here." He may have meant to sound funny, but there was an edge to his voice.

Park wondered if he should say something. He tried out a few phrases in his head. How are things? Has the baby come yet? How's the missus? Guess what happened while you were gone today?

"I need to get right back to the hospital. So I want you all to slop the pigs, all right?"

"Okay, no worry."

"If the creamery calls, I'm dropping the can off on the way to the hospital. I told Mrs. Davenport in case they call the big house. I also told her, Thanh, that I want you to spend the night there tonight. It's set and I don't want you fussing about it."

"Okay, okay. I no fuss. Oooo. Full of prickle."

If Frank heard her muttered complaint, he ignored it. "And eat your supper, for heaven's sake. It's not going to kill you to eat her cooking one night."

"Who know? Just might kill."

"And be polite about it."

"Okay, okay. We little angel girl. We help our poor, tired mommy and nice Mr. Frank. We put napkin on lap. We no kick table. We don't slosh no soy sauce on nothing." Her imitation of Mrs. Davenport made Park burrow his face in the cow's flank to keep from snickering aloud. "We eat our vegetable. We eat our meat. Even can't tell which thing meat which thing vegetable. We eat. Yum yum. Thank you, Mrs. Davenport. So good. So delicious meal—"

"Thanh, okay. That's enough. Just behave yourself, okay?"

"You ask her behave?"

"Please, Thanh. Just help me tonight, all right? There's a lot going on—I don't have any idea when I'll get back—"

"My mama okay?" Her voice had gone suddenly serious with a little tremble in it.

"The doctor says she's doing fine. It's just taking longer than we hoped. She'll be all right. I'm sure she'll be fine. I just don't want her to have to worry about how you're behaving."

There was no saucy comeback. Park listened through the sounds of milk hitting milk, the restless swish and stomp of the cows. Was she crying? He couldn't be sure. Frank should be more patient with her. He didn't have to take his anxieties out on her.

She was very quiet at supper. Once when Mrs. Davenport had gone into the kitchen, Park looked at his plate and mouthed across to Thanh, "Which thing meat? Which thing vegetable?" She smiled wanly.

"Excuse," she said when the plates were reasonably empty, "must go get night clothes."

Park jumped up. "I'll help," he said. Both Mrs. Davenport and Thanh gave him a look. "Carry your suitcase or something," he said, feeling a little foolish.

"Your mother's all right. I know she is," he said to Thanh as they circled the vegetable garden on the way down to the little house.

"You think?"

"Oh, I'm sure. Babies always take a long time coming."

"Not always. I see in camp. Poop. Quick as nothing."

"It always takes longer in a hospital."

"So? Seem crazy."

"Yeah, I know. But that's the way it is."

She stopped walking and looked at him. "I think you don't know nothing about baby come. You just say. Right?"

"Well, I don't think you need to worry. Frank's all upset because it's his first baby. He doesn't know anything either."

"Mens," she said, shaking her head and starting toward the house again. "Every men I know crazy. Even Frank sometime."

141

She opened the door and switched on a light. Park followed her in. Had Frank brought all the books down from the big house? It was a family of crazy men. She was right. Books and cows and war. They didn't seem to go together.

"Can I use your phone?"

She shrugged toward the kitchen. "You call telephone. I get giant suitcase, too heavy for poor little Thanh," she said, going down toward her room.

"Mom?"

"Just a minute, please." The aggravating operator. "I have a call from—"

"Yes, I'll take it. Pork? What is it? Are you all right?"

"I'm fine. I just needed—" Where to begin? "Mom, why didn't you tell me you and my dad were divorced?"

"I was going to."

"Well, you're a little late. Mom, it's not the kind of thing you want to be told by someone you just met who happens to be your father's brother only you never knew he existed—"

"You mustn't blame Frank." Who was blaming Frank? Cripes. "It's not Frank's fault. It's no fun going through your life mopping up someone else's mess."

"Is that what you think Thanh is?"

"What?"

"Not *what*, Mom, *who*. She happens to be my sister."

"Oh, Pork. Did Frank—?"

"No, I figured it out for myself."

Her familiar sigh. "He thought I'd understand." At first Park thought she meant Frank; then he realized she meant his dad. "He told me about—about this woman over there. I guess he wanted me to say it didn't matter. That it had nothing to do with us. But, Park, it did matter. I couldn't

142

pretend—" She stopped a minute. "When I couldn't—I guess the word is *forgive,* although that makes me sound like I thought I was God, which I certainly never did—anyhow, when I couldn't— You can't understand, you're too young, you've never loved somebody the way— He was my whole life."

Park waited. He wanted to tell her it was okay. He wanted to stop her pain, but he didn't. He just waited, not speaking, until she went on.

"Anyhow, when I—when I couldn't understand how he could do what he did, he went back. And then he died." The pitch of her voice had risen. Park tried not to imagine her face, her eyes. "He never gave me a second chance. He died."

"But you divorced him first."

"Oh, baby, try to understand. I had to be a person by myself. I couldn't depend— I couldn't let him, let anybody be my whole life." She was quiet again. Park couldn't tell if she was crying. "Anyhow, I guess I thought he'd stop me."

Thanh was standing now half in the room, her body holding the swinging door ajar. "I gotta go," he said. "Thanks for—" What did he want to thank her for?

"I never understood why Frank let her come over here. Hadn't she done enough damage? I can't understand that. And then he marries her, for God's sake. Why would he do that?"

"I don't know, Mom," he said. Thanh had put her head into the refrigerator and was taking things out. She stuck something into his mouth. It was a kind of egg roll. Cold, but not bad tasting.

"You okay, bud?" his mother was asking.

He took the egg roll out of his mouth. "I'm okay, Mom. How 'bout you?"

"I'll be okay. And Park—" She'd called him by his dad's name.

"Yes, Mom?"

"I'll be glad to see you. I miss you."

"I miss you too, Mom," he said as gently as he knew how.

At about nine the phone rang. They were watching television in the dining room. Mrs. Davenport looked hopefully first at Park and then at Thanh.

Both of them stood up. "I get," said Thanh. Park took a step or two toward the kitchen, trying to hear. Yes, apparently the baby had come. "Okay. Okay," Thanh repeated. "Okay. Nice. Good. Yeah, I fine. Okay. Sure. Okay."

"Well?" Park asked when she hung up.

"Bruzzuh," she muttered. "Now two big fat stupid bruzzuh."

"What's that?" called Mrs. Davenport. "Do we have some news?"

"It's a boy," Park said.

He waited until he was sure Mrs. Davenport was asleep. Then he crept out of his room and down the hall to the room where Thanh was staying. He rapped gently. "Thanh?"

She opened it at once. "Okay," she said. "I got bread already from my house and hamburger. He like hamburger." She didn't say how she knew, but Park was not in a position to argue. He had never been on speaking acquaintance with a crow before.

At the top of the stairs he glanced nervously at the door to Mrs. Davenport's room. "Not worry," Thanh whispered, raising her eyebrows. "We sleep like potato."

They tiptoed down the steps and were about to open the

door into the back hall when they heard the *thump*-shuffling sound. She looked questioningly at Park. "Grandfather," he whispered. "I think he practices walking at night."

"Oh my good," she said.

They listened a minute longer. Now they could hear soft crying as well as the *thump* and shuffle. "He cry," she whispered.

Park nodded.

He opened his mouth to protest, but she was already in the room. "Hello. No cry. We take you ride. Okay?" She was pushing the wheelchair up behind the old man. "You help!" she commanded Park in a very loud whisper.

The old man looked as astonished as Park felt, but he sat down heavily in the wheelchair Thanh had slipped under his hips. Park got the bathrobe off a hook on the door and, half lifting the old man, put it on him and eased him back into the chair.

"Move thing." Thanh shoved Park aside and took the handles of the chair, waving at Park to get the walker.

"Hold up a minute, Thanh. I got to get him covered." He fetched the afghan from an armchair and tied the bathrobe sash and tucked the afghan around the old man's lap and legs before he moved the walker and let Thanh push the chair out the door.

They took the chair through the back hall and across the porch. "What about Jupe?" He was still whispering. "Will he bark?"

She shrugged, so he went out the screen door first and called quietly. "Jupe. Here, Jupe."

He could see the dog coming toward him in the moonlight. "Okay, he's here. Now. Turn the chair around. Let's back him off the porch. I better get his head. It's heavier."

With Park easing the wheels down over the stoop and Thanh holding on to the footrests, they were able to get the chair off the porch with only a minor jolt.

"Okay?" Thanh asked the old man.

Park turned the chair around and started slowly toward the gate. Once out of the yard, Thanh tried once more to take over the pushing.

"He like fast," she said. "Don't you like fast?"

"No," Park said. "Not tonight. It's dark. We gotta see where we're going."

"Yellow chicken," she said amicably, shrugging an apology to the old man, and then, with Jupe frolicking around her legs, she danced ahead of them down the road. As the path dropped off more steeply, Park had to hold back to keep the chair from racing downhill. In the moonlight he felt as though he were following fairy shadows. He wondered if the old man sensed the enchantment.

By the time they got to the gate, she was standing there, holding it open. "What I do," she said. "I go get water. Take to crow. Get gun. You wait at spring. Okay?"

He was relieved that she didn't expect him to push the chair uphill and down to the far pasture, but—to wait alone with the old man? His heart began to pound faster. He licked his lips. "Okay," he said. "Sure."

Jupe looked at the girl and then at the chair, as though torn. When he realized that she was going and they were staying, he gave a yelp of delight and raced after her.

Now they were truly alone. Park turned the chair so the old man could see the moon, and set the brake. He started to sit down on the grass. It was damp, so he sat on his haunches Thanh-style a few feet from the chair. The afghan had come loose in the trip down the hill. He went over and squatted in front of the chair and began to tuck it close around the old pajamaed legs.

"Haaaa." There was nowhere to run. His heart had stopped, but Park made himself look up into the old face. Even in the shadows, he thought he could see tears. "Haaaa."

"What's the matter?" Park willed the words out of his mouth. "Does something hurt?"

The clawlike left hand came out from under the afghan and reached toward him. Park held himself tightly so as not to flinch, not to retreat. The back of the hand touched Park's cheek, then fell away. With an effort, the old man lifted the hand again. This time it went back and forth several times, cool and baby soft against Park's face. "Haaaa," he repeated. "Haaaa." The hand flopped heavily from Park's cheek to his own chest.

"Yes," said Park, suddenly understanding. "Park. You mean Park. I'm Park, and you're Park. That's what you mean, right?"

His grandfather turned his twisted head slightly, as if to nod, then repeated the stroke of Park's cheek and the touch of his own breast with gentle *haaaa*'s each time.

"Yes, we're both Park." Park could understand him! He was, if not making conversation, at least making contact with his grandfather. He wanted to grab the old hands or hug the old body. Suddenly the withered arm was flung out toward the sky.

"HAAAAAA!" the old man sobbed out. "HAAAAAAA!" The arm fell lifeless to the side of the chair. There was no question now about the tears.

"What is it?" Park was crying too. "What is it? Do you miss him? Is that it?" But the pain in the eyes said more than grief.

"Don't cry, please don't cry." Park hugged the old knees. The sobbing did not lessen.

"What is it?" He stood up and took the wasted face between his hands and held it. His grandfather's tears wet his fingers. The tears were running down his own cheeks, too, catching in his glasses. He let them run. "What's the matter? Please tell me," he begged. And now, looking into the eyes, he saw his mother's eyes and his own eyes, as in a mirror. So that was it. "You think you killed him," Park said softly. "You think it's your fault."

Between his fingers, he could feel his grandfather's head move forward and back. He was nodding yes.

Park let the face go and put his arms around his grandfather's shoulders and held him tight while they both cried like lost three-year-olds returned at last to their mothers' arms.

"Gone!" Thanh was yelling as she ran down the road, waving his bloodstained T-shirt above her head. "Gone!"

"Gone?" Not their crow. Not dead. Not now. "What happened?"

"Okay!" she cried. "Okay. Fly free!"

She threw him the T-shirt and ran past them into the springhouse. When she came out, it was slowly, carrying in both hands the coconut shell, filled to overflowing with cool, sweet water. "Now," she ordered. "Now. All drink."

Then they took the Holy Grail in their hands and drew away the cloth and drank of the Holy Wine. And it seemed to all who saw them that their faces shone with a light that was not of this world. And they were as one in the company of the Grail.

ACKNOWLEDGMENTS

For their help, witting or unwitting, I should like to thank: Roger Lancelyn Green, Samuel Hutchins, Jean Little, Claire Mackay, Thomas Malory, Joanna Macy, Kathryn Morton, Alex and Joan Sarjeant, Mark Sassi, Mary Lee Settle, Dick Shaw, Rosemary Sutcliff, Raymond Thomas, Wolfram von Eschenbach, Cora and Florence Womeldorf, and, as always, John Paterson.

ABOUT THE AUTHOR

KATHERINE PATERSON's books have received wide acclaim and been published in many languages. Among them are *Come Sing, Jimmy Jo,* an ALA Notable Children's Book; *Rebels of the Heavenly Kingdom*; and *Gates of Excellence.* Others include *Jacob Have I Loved* and *Bridge to Terabithia,* winners of the 1981 and 1978 Newbery Medals; *The Great Gilly Hopkins,* a Newbery Honor Book and winner of the 1979 National Book Award; and *The Master Puppeteer,* which received the 1977 National Book Award.

The parents of four children, Mrs. Paterson and her husband live in Barre, Vermont.